THE HOUSE OF CHILDHOOD

Marie Luise Kaschnitz

Das Haus der Kindheit

Translated by Anni Whissen

Afterword by Hal H. Rennert

The House
of
Childhood

*University
of
Nebraska Press*

*Lincoln
&
London*

Copyright © 1990
    by the University of Nebraska Press
All rights reserved
    Manufactured in the United States
of America
    Originally published as *Das Haus
der Kindheit,* © 1956 by
    Claassen Verlag GmbH, Hamburg
The paper in this book
    meets the minimum requirements
of American National
    Standard for Information Sciences –
Permanence of Paper
    for Printed Library Materials,
ANSI Z39.46-1984.
    Library of Congress Cataloging in
Publication Data
    Kaschnitz, Marie Luise, 1901-1974.
[Haus der Kindheit. English]
    The House of Childhood / by Marie
Luise Kaschnitz : translated
    by Anni Whissen : afterword by
Hal H. Rennert.
        p.   cm.–(European women writers
series) Trans-
        lation of: Das Haus der Kindheit.
ISBN 0-8032-2723-X (alk. paper).–
    ISBN 0-8032-7773-3 (pbk: alk. paper)
I. Title.   II. Series.
    PT2621.A73H3813   1990
833'.912–dc20 90–31858 CIP

Contents

THE HOUSE OF CHILDHOOD

To My Sisters and Brother

I

It all began when a stranger stopped me on the street and asked me a question. He asked if I knew the city well and if I could tell him where the House of Childhood was. What's that supposed to be, I asked surprised, a museum? I don't think so, the man said. Maybe a school, I continued, or a kindergarten? The man shrugged. I don't know, he said. He had gray hair and looked sort of provincial. To help him, I put my glasses on and read some of the inscriptions on the houses nearby. Conservatory, it said, Movie Theater, Life Insurance Co. There wasn't anything like a House of Childhood, and I certainly had never heard of it. Why are you looking for this house, I asked, trying to get a clue. I've got business there, the man said, I'm getting old. He politely tipped his hat and left. I walked on, thinking about this last somewhat puzzling remark of his and turned down the wrong street out of sheer absentmindedness. After I'd walked a few hundred paces, I saw the House.

2

Naturally I hurried back immediately that day to tell the

stranger what I'd found out, but he was already out of sight. That's not particularly unusual since our city is pretty big and full of people, especially around noon. Furthermore, since the war many blocks have been so completely reconstructed that you don't know your way around anymore and sometimes don't even know exactly where you are. A number of public buildings have also been built, including some that didn't exist before at all and which serve the particular needs of our times. I assume that this so-called House of Childhood is among those postwar accomplishments. As far as I could tell in my hurry, it was a big gray building without any special adornment except for a kind of Jugendstil embellishment placed above the portal and below which the name was written in golden letters.

3

I have no reason at all, of course, to find out anything about the building this stranger was looking for, or even to go back there again for a closer look. As a matter of fact, I've even started having doubts about whether or not I really read the inscription correctly since I'm rather nearsighted and actually can't read print at all from where I was standing at the time. But today, from my dressmaker's window, I saw the House again, this time, so it seemed, from the rear. I recognized it by its gray stone which has something oddly impermanent, almost theater-like about it. And I realized for the first time that the windows of the strange house were walled up. I asked my dressmaker about the building, but since she had just recently moved into her apartment, she couldn't tell me anything.

4

Today when I was visiting some friends, we talked about the increased construction in our city and about what conveniences and possibilities for spiritual enrichment the taxpayer is offered these days. There was mention not only of escalators, pools, public libraries, and children's playgrounds but also of various new collections and educational centers like the cosmetics museum, the exhibit "What's Barking There?" and the Shakespeare underwater theater. I took the opportunity to tell them about the House of Childhood, and they all showed a great deal of interest. Some of them wanted to have a look at this new center with me, and we decided on a day and a time when we could all go. But as I was leaving, I realized that I had not noted the name of the street I'd taken by mistake. We decided that I should go there alone first and then phone my friends.

5

I've postponed my visit to the children's museum, or whatever it may be, until next week because I've been swamped with work. In the meantime, of course, I could have tried to walk past by myself on, say, an errand to town, but I probably also would have lost a good deal of time doing so. I'm pretty sure now that the street in which the building was located was a cul-de-sac. I remember a high gray wall blocking the way at the end of the street, making it impossible to get past the House to other parts of town. It's quite possible that the visitor who takes the entire tour is let out through another exit. After all, given the long-windedness of museum guides, it's easy for a tour like that to take several hours.

6

The thing is that the mere word *childhood* makes me kind of nervous. It's amazing how little I remember from my childhood and how much I dislike being reminded of that time by others. Whereas a series of bright, happy pictures appear in most people's minds, there is in my case simply a black hole that makes me sad whenever I peer into it. I suppose this lack of memory has a definite cause. Besides, every thought of the past simply leaves a bad taste in my mouth. That's why I'm glad I haven't visited the House of Childhood. Probably it doesn't contain anything other than a collection of toys and picture books, just like the ones you see in the store windows. Maybe there's also a record collection, and you can have Christmas carols and nursery rhymes played on request, things that seem to possess a certain folkloric value in a day and age when our cultural heritage is swiftly disappearing. Something like that could be done very nicely, I'm sure, but in any case it's not for me.

7

Apparently the House of Childhood is located much closer to my apartment than I thought. I suddenly found myself standing in front of it today and took the opportunity to study it carefully. To the right of the big front door there was a flat white doorbell and a pane of opaque glass, also a mouthpiece that you could talk into. I once saw such a device in one of our new municipal offices. As soon as you ring the bell, you hear a polite male voice: "Please announce yourself. State your name and date of birth." I was convinced that it was a similar system here. The pane of opaque glass is most likely part of a camera that transmits a life-size picture of me somewhere in the interior of the House the moment I get close to it. Things of that sort remind me of the Gestapo and disgust me. Naturally I left without ringing the bell.

8

Talked to Carl about the museum and about going over there. I had to describe everything to him, and he was especially interested in the institutionally boring character of the architecture and the walled-up windows. The absurd idea occurred to us that the contents of the House are not permanent but are changed for every visitor as soon as one's arrival is announced. In that case you could not expect picture books, toys, and children's furniture of a general nature but rather the most personal things. It would then be completely impossible for more than one person to be admitted at the same time. Too bad. With Carl at my side, I really could have gotten a lot of enjoyment out of the new establishment.

9

It's strange that as soon as you have a specific subject in mind, everybody starts talking about things that are related to this same subject without even being asked. Time and again I meet people now whose faces grow dark at the thought of their childhoods although they apparently neither went hungry nor were mistreated as children. On the other hand, the visit to the childhood museum is being urged upon me by completely different people, without their being aware of it, of course. For example, today it was Eve who insisted that at some time in life one would *have to* deal with one's childhood; it might be unpleasant perhaps, but there was no way around it. I doubt that she's right; anyway, it's not the case with me. I don't have any particular problems that could be solved by means of this type of exploration of the past, and whenever they refer to my age as a critical age, I usually say there's no age that's not critical in some way or other. I'm in the fortunate position of still being loved and, what's more important, of still being able to feel that love. When I look in the mirror, I'm overcome with a certain gallows humor that I hope will linger till I no longer care at all about external things.

10

Today I copied down here all entries having to do with the museum from my regular diary which, of course, contains many other, completely different items. After all, it could be that I really might go over there and that I would then be motivated to describe the museum in detail. These notes would take up an extraordinary amount of space in my diary, and I would later be tempted to ascribe to them an importance that they don't deserve. For when all is said and done, the only thing that's important is the present. We are powerless in the face of the past; it is a dead substance that we cannot change and that cannot come alive anymore.

11

Admission to the museum is free, as it says on a plaque near the front door. Of course, that just means that you don't have to pay with money, and that hardly means anything. I can easily imagine being robbed of my freedom in the House of Childhood; the use of modern methods of subjugating your will, like floodlights or drugs, is also quite conceivable. They've always said about old people that they become childish. It may well be that once you've begun to feel at home in the House, you'll give in to its spell and won't be able to get along in the outside world anymore. That thought frightens me, just as I'm getting more and more repelled by the whole idea of a childhood museum.

12

I've made a frightening discovery. The House moves. When I looked out the window this evening, albeit in a state of great exhaustion, I didn't see the little familiar piece of lawn with the clothesline and the lilac bushes already bare, but something quite different that told me right away that it formed a part of the mysterious House or that it had emerged from it. I won't describe what I saw, because I take it to be a hallucination that I'll do my best to forget. Every human being is subject to that kind of hallucination; it just depends on what powers of resistance you have to counter it. My philosophy of always carrying out well – in fact, in the best way possible – whatever has to be done really comes in handy here.

13

Thought about the strange sight I saw yesterday and faced the possibility that it might appear again. It would probably be better to go visit the House voluntarily rather than to end up as a victim of its strange tricks. Free will is a mighty weapon. Those who make use of it are in an entirely different position from those who are pushed or pulled; more than anything, they go just as far as they want to, and it's up to them to put an end to the adventure as soon as they've had enough. Please just show me the most important rooms, I would say; as a matter of fact, I don't have much time. Actually, I'm only interested in having a quick look.

14

November days with falling leaves that make all my friends melancholy. A singer down in the courtyard (an endangered species that should be described in detail) was singing the song about the ancestral grave while winter coals were being dumped on the street from a truck and then shoveled into the cellar. I was feeling great. Fall doesn't get me down. All you have to do is spend a little time with botany to know that next year's buds are already formed at this time. Besides, nothing is more beautiful than trees going dormant in the fall or tulip calyxes forming husks. At least it's better than the so-called attractions of early spring with its false starts and lackluster sheen.

15

The sudden death of an acquaintance has upset our whole circle of friends. In addition to the personal loss, the manner of death – the completely unexpected cessation of breathing – has left a frightening impression. That is understandable where devout Catholics are concerned, but actually it was precisely those others, the nonbelievers, who were most horrified. It seemed to me that they felt most sorry for the deceased because he had not had time to take stock, that is, to settle in his own mind which things in life had been worth living for. Maybe, someone thought, there were dark areas in his life, as in all lives, that he might have wanted to clear up or knots that he might have wanted to untie. I found these concerns petty and unsuitable. They say that when a man plunges from a roof, his whole life passes before his eyes in a flash and in every detail – so apparently it takes only a few seconds to come to terms with oneself.

16

In the wonderful travels of little Nils Holgersson, the boy who was transformed into a dwarf pays with a lowly copper coin in the bazaars of the lost city of Vineta, or rather he was supposed to pay with it and save the whole submerged city that way. It is quite possible that those most wonderful means of payment may also be good in the House of Childhood, in fact, that the whole museum consists of automated peep shows whose pictures cannot be viewed at all without the proper coin or the correct magic word. In any case, you pay, in a figurative sense, with life, with the present, in other words with the most valuable thing you've got.

17

Haven't thought about the House for several days. In the newspapers there's been a lot of talk about atomic energy, which seems to be ushering in a new age for man just now. The extreme danger surrounding this discovery lends something strangely impersonal to everything connected with it; its cosmic nature makes the individual human life insignificant and small. To go looking for one's own past seems absolutely absurd, even childish, in this context. I can't grasp the fact that, at the very moment when there are so many more important things to be done, our city would produce a means of parading before the eyes of every inhabitant his or her most insignificant childhood with a contrivance that apparently is both complicated and expensive. But in the final analysis, I don't know the first thing about it. It might all be much more modest and finally nothing more than a minor pastime.

18

What happened recently occurred again. I had something to drop off at a place that I don't know very well and got into a conversation with the lady of the house. We were standing in the front room. The kids were running through the room to the back yard, among them a little girl dressed like a warrior with sticks and ropes and a wild Indian headdress. "My daughter never plays with dolls," the mother said laughing, although there was a trace of concern in her voice. At that moment, the room around me underwent an instant transformation although no other room of any definite shape emerged. I kind of lost the ground under my feet; in the place of pleasant and rational conversation came words and chaotic snatches of sound. Although I've never set foot in the House of Childhood, I'm nevertheless convinced that at this moment it was seizing hold of me again and even more powerfully than the first time. I'm determined not to put up with it anymore. In fact, I might just

9

go over there and protest against this kind of harassment from afar, which surely must be punishable by law.

19

It's boring always to use the full designation for the strange House when I think about it and write about it. For all public institutions they now use abbreviations formed by combining the initial letters of the individual words. These acronyms often have something funny and intimate about them that seems to belie the institutions they stand for (banks, department stores, offices, etc.). As soon as you pronounce them, you establish a new and more harmless relationship with the institution in question. There's something fresh and adventurous about the word *H.O.C.*, for instance, that cheers me up and gives me courage. Besides, since I made it up myself, it belongs to me and allows me to gain power over the subject in question, at least to some extent.

20

Straightened up the apartment. Discovered some suspicious articles, suspicious since I believe they can be found in the H.O.C. in the same or in a similar style. I've removed these items. Nevertheless, a feeling of uneasiness or, actually, vague discontent remains. I wonder why. I feel as if I'm gradually losing much of my self-confidence. I've got to get over there.

21

It's interesting that the H.O.C. is not advertised in any way. Neither in the want ads of the newspaper nor on the movie screen is there the slightest hint of this new possibility of furthering one's education or gaining certain insight. No one talks about it, and those friends of mine whom I told about it a few weeks ago and who wanted to go with me have never brought up this plan again. It would be my guess that the House exists, if not solely for me, then at least for a fairly limited number of persons, namely for those who, like me, have no memories or are unwilling to remember. If that's the case, then perhaps we're talking about a kind of clinic, an institution for the treatment of abnormal cases. Since that thought occurred to me, the H.O.C. has become totally repulsive to me. I have no interest whatsoever in the methods of modern psychology. I'm in the best of health.

22

I don't care much for the designation H.O.C. It reminds me of certain stores that offer wholesale articles at fixed prices. I have always hated those stores, especially because of their smell, which makes you feel sick to your stomach from the hodge-podge of toilet articles, rubber, food items, and body odors. Aside from this association, the acronym H.O.C. is also too transparent, too revealing for my purposes. I would like to be in a position to mention the House without feeling the undeniable hold it is beginning to exert over me.

23

Today I glanced into the interior of the strange museum complex for the first time. It was all very easy. A gate in the wall, which I had already noticed the first time I walked through the street but which had been closed on that occasion, was open today, just a crack. However, without anyone noticing I was able to widen the crack far enough to see what was behind the wall. To describe what I saw is difficult, to say the least. The most important thing, it seems to me, is to say that the impression I had earlier of something theatrical was fully confirmed. The whole layout is a stage set, the building itself only a facade, nothing more. Behind the facade and out in the open are a number of structures that are hard to identify – structures of the kind you might find on the lots of a movie studio, also little gardens and woods so natural looking that I couldn't tell whether they were real or just fashioned artificially from wood, fabric, or cardboard. The most confusing thing about seeing all these things was that from several machines hidden from view the most extraordinary light, indeed, even one deep artificial shadow, was falling on them like the dark of night. The whole thing seemed disorderly, even chaotic, but not at all sinister, and when I left, I had to laugh when I thought how afraid I had been before the visit to the place and how I had been postponing it for such a long time.

24

The first hard frost. On the windowpanes the most beautiful ice crystals that you recognize year after year as a magic reawakening of fossilized flora. I'd been planning for quite some time to describe in detail these gardens from the youth of mankind. Descriptions of that nature, of course, belong in my other diary. I just had it out and noticed to my amazement that I'd made no entries since October 10. Just think how much time I've lost with all this philosophizing about the House of Childhood. I'm happy that I know now what it's all about. Now I'm free.

25

Of course, I don't really know anything except that the museum has not yet been completed. In the old days, when construction ceased during the winter months, it would probably not have been finished for quite a while. But nowadays they put up buildings using artificial heating of the materials and electric light. When I go over there again in a few weeks, I'll probably notice considerable progress. It's quite clear to me that they're aspiring to have the most advanced instructional techniques. Of course, they can only be commended on that. You often wonder, for example, what minimal use schools make of resources like film, radio, and television. I wouldn't consider it out of the question that our city, by contrast, might be retaining certain especially characteristic recordings and pictures from the childhood of every individual citizen.

26

Followed the cul-de-sac to its end again. This time the gate was closed, but I did discover a kind of antiquated firing slit in the wall, which, incidentally, much to my surprise, narrowed toward the side facing the street just as if it were a matter of defending the outside rather than the inside. The slit was very narrow, but nevertheless I could see that nothing had changed at all since my last visit. The same deserted lot with its countless indistinguishable structures, the same woods and gardens, only this time the lighting was missing; in fact, a gray, cold fog shrouded the strange objects. This sight made me change my mind completely about the fact that it was a museum under construction. The facade of the House may very well be a ruin left over from the war whereas the structures behind it probably are a part of a fantastic venture once planned and since abandoned. I'm only too familiar with such ventures. In the newspapers that I write for, I myself am quite used to bringing such matters to the attention of the public. I need only think of the mysterious hotel where all the windows face an interior courtyard landscaped with evergreens, or of the wax museums with their historical figures that are to be placed behind glass

along the subway, items that suit my own peculiar require-
ments and of which the public lacks any proper understanding.

27

Dreams have the strangest way of bringing past events, even
dead issues to life again. For example, I dreamed the other
night about a meadow that, as I fully realized in the dream, was
located in the House of Childhood. A tiny brook flowed
through the meadow. The grasses growing at its edge were
flooded with water, which caused them to bend and emerge
again, crowned with drops that glistened in the sunshine like
fabulous jewels. I was overcome with a deep feeling of happiness, and, to tell the truth, it was not the happiness of an ob-
server but rather of a participant, just as if I myself were the water or the grass. When I woke up, I was firmly convinced that
the House did indeed exist and that it was perfectly capable of
transmitting experiences other than those that are unpleasant
and humiliating. When I go over there again, it's possible that
the firing slit will be walled up and that the gate will have disappeared, but then there'll still be the front door, the bell, the
mouthpiece, and the pane of opaque glass. I can just imagine
how the doorman will get a kick out of my surprise when I open
the door and step not into any interior room but rather out into
the open again. But, of course, I'm not at all surprised. I know.

28

The strange building site still holds an attraction for me. I've
found out that the few stores that are located in the cul-de-sac
are not bad at all, and I have decided to do some of my shop-
ping there. In the grocery store you can get things that you can't
get anywhere else anymore, for example, coarse spelt which is a
wheat product from the region I come from and which makes

wonderful soups. Although I don't eat sweets, I enjoy looking at the chocolates and confections in the window of a coffee shop that bears the curious name of Zuntz's Late Widow. The clerks in the stores are very friendly, and you feel you've known them for the longest time. A couple of days ago, I finally discovered at the very end of the street a coffeehouse with dusty plush sofas and piles of newspapers. It was very quiet there, and I went back the next day to write my newspaper articles. Maybe I'll start doing all my work there. The ventilation is poor, but there's no phone, and I'm sure none of my friends ever go there. Needless to say, I also hope to get information about the adjoining lot from the waiter, who in accordance with a tradition long since forgotten keeps bringing me glasses of fresh water.

29

Have asked the waiter. He didn't know anything, and he showed very little interest in the matter. He advised me to ring the bell on the museum door and to wait to see if anyone would even show up. In the meantime, I've made myself at home at a table in the corner. I can even leave my books there. Few people seem to frequent the place. At the newspaper, which I have to contact once in a while, I've left word that I'm taking a trip, that I'll be somewhere out in the country. Actually, it's not the time of year to be in the country. Those who want to get away from it all are off to Egypt or to the new artificial oases that are popping up in ever greater numbers in the Sahara. But in any case, it's a good idea to get away from one's familiar surroundings. Even at this very moment, I feel as if I'm on vacation.

30

Heard a lecture on Indian religions and the belief in the transmigration of souls. Aside from the interesting comparison of nirvana with the recently popular and notorious nothingness of the French existentialists, I'm occupying myself more than anything with the thought of how upsetting it must be to accept an earlier existence as a fait accompli and not to have the faintest notion of what this past life was like. I imagine that orthodox Hindus occasionally try to find out what surroundings they once lived in, what they looked like, and what unique characteristics they might have had. Since these people constantly strive to evolve spiritually – and this desire for evolution applies to their place in the caste system as well – the knowledge of previous mistakes would have to be of particular importance to them. I don't rule out the possibility that the methods of such an inquiry into the past will be refined some day (on the order of the childhood museum) and that they eventually will lead to the desired goal.

31

I didn't hear any power drills or cement mixers all week as I sat in the coffeehouse writing my articles; in fact, I wasn't aware of any construction noise at all. And yet, as I hurried down the street on a sudden impulse and rang the doorbell to the museum, I found that one room had already been completed. It was a long, narrow room, like the ones used for showing slides or films in schools or universities. It was dark, and I didn't pay any attention to whether it was equipped with rows of chairs or not. As soon as I had stepped in off the street, I was drawn to a picture that appeared on the narrow wall across from me. The picture showed a man and a dog . . .

32

I couldn't get any writing done yesterday. The waiter kept bothering me. He doesn't have anything to do, so he gets nosy.

He wanted to know the titles of some of my latest essays: "The Supernatural Age," "Atom and Eroticism," etc., and he kept shaking his head in amazement. I told him nothing about what I had just seen in the House. I have the distinct impression that it was designed for me and for me only. Actually, I need only close my eyes to see the whole scene clearly outlined before me. The man is holding on with both hands to a leather strap or other coarse material which the dog, a small, strong bulldog, has got its fangs into. The man raises his arms and keeps turning around and around in a rage. The dog won't let go and is swung around in a circle three feet above the ground. There's something strained and desperate about its eyes, and they are full of blood. The room is dark, man and dog give off their own ccric light while turning faster and faster.

33

What is the point of these presentations that appear to be about memories of early childhood, I wonder? The business of the dog, for instance, didn't help me much, it merely confused me. At least they ought to have someone there to explain such images. I looked around for someone like that today but didn't find anyone. And, by the way, even the projection room wasn't there any longer. Although I walked in through the same door, the main entrance, I found myself in a kind of dressing room today and opposite a large mirror. In this mirror I saw myself, only distorted, my own large and horribly aged face on a delicate child's body. Those kinds of mirrors are still to be found at fairs sometimes, where they can be a lot of fun when you look into them with people who are out to have a good time. They seem appropriate in an amusement park but are completely out of place in an institution of learning. Visitors to a museum not only wish to take things seriously, they also wish to be taken seriously themselves. They feel repulsed and offended in an institution like this.

34

The impression of disorder and lack of seriousness of purpose that I had when I first visited the House has increased. As if it were just a matter of flimsy movie sets, to be used only briefly, there's always just one room available, behind whose walls one senses a terrible chaos. I might add that these sets also include a bit of nature, like a courtyard or a garden, as the case may warrant. On this order, the annex I was in today had a small courtyard shaded by chestnut trees, soft sunlight, and the green shadows of chestnut leaves moving on the sidewalk like small hands. In the middle of the annex, a little old lady was singing in a trembly voice. Her hands were not green but white; she held them high with spread-out fingers and kept turning them in front of my face. "Ainsi font, font, font les petites marionettes," she sang. Then she stopped, only to continue at a faster pace, "Trois petits tours et puis s'en vont," at which her hands swiftly disappeared behind her back like fluttering doves.

35

Ran into Carl on the street. He wanted to take me home, but since I was on my way to the coffeehouse, I turned down his offer. I wouldn't want him to find out about my current hideout, where he might come looking for me some day. I fear his visit would be inconvenient and that I might let on that he's in the way. I wonder if he remembers what I told him once about the House of Childhood. Maybe so. At any rate, I'm very grateful to him for not mentioning it. I told him today that I was very busy and that I would call him as soon as I had gotten my work off my back, which actually is the truth. We chatted for a while, and although I was glad that he seemed to be fine, I had for the first time in his presence the feeling of precious time slipping away. When I turned around once more as I was leaving, I noticed his glance directed at me, full of concern, the way you look at someone who's ill and doesn't want to be taken care of.

36

That scene with the old lady made a pleasant impression on me. Presumably because it was more or less complete in spite of the fact that it made no sense. During my visits yesterday and today, there was no trace of such completeness, and I have the impression that experiences of this sort are not at all the rule. In general, the format seems to be that you either see or hear or smell or taste something. Yesterday, for example, I heard in a dark room one single scream that went right through me, and today I blindly ran into a veil of iron, hurting my lips, while smelling powder and the fragrance of violets. The senses are separated from one another as it were, through which process each one seems to be sharpened and made particularly receptive. The urgency of impressions like that is almost painful, maybe even more so because you don't just pass from one to the next but are forced to experience, I might almost say practice, each one several times. Five or six times in succession, the scream without any additional sounds reverberating in the air, just as many times the quiet scratching of the veil on my lips; behind that, dead cold, as from fog-shrouded skin.

37

I've made it a point to visit the House at a certain time every day. I go in the mornings at around eleven after I've had breakfast in the coffee house, read the papers, and organized the work I have to get done for that day. There's no need to establish the duration of the visit, as I've noticed; you're in no way detained but rather dismissed every time, sometimes even after a few minutes. What is important, on the other hand, is to determine the time itself, because that way something rational, you might almost say something human, is set off against the disorderly and rather casual atmosphere that exists in the museum. For the first time in my life, I'm happy to have a watch, especially because there is no clock in the coffeehouse. This is even more astounding since everything else there is completely normal, in fact, almost ordinary in a spooky kind of way. Grayish brown lace curtains, a potted palm, couches with wooden arms, lots of plush. You can find similar restaurants in Vienna to this day, somewhere in the Währing district I believe, where they're still frequented by older people on occasion but totally ignored by the younger generation.

38

It's hard to put into words what you may find in the House sometimes, I mean, no surroundings at all, no sounds, no smells, no pictures. Something happens with one, to one, events of a petty, downright humiliating kind. Since I hate to recollect these things, I'll summarize briefly what happened to me during my last visit. First item: I fall flat on my face, and with full force at that. My body hits the ground, which is hard as a rock, my mouth is full of dust and my eyes full of flying sparks, I can't catch my breath. As I try sitting up, a shadowy and utterly strange world keeps turning before my eyes. I'm released from my own body and simply lost – my first new breath requires a terrible, destructive energy on my part. Second item: I've hardly entered before they push something into my mouth that tastes like a dried-up sandwich. As I start to chew, I bite my tongue. My teeth are sharp, my mouth is a wound, the violent pain shoots through my body in waves. I'm forced to howl like an animal and scare myself more than anyone. Third item: I feel sick to my stomach. Probably I have eaten too much, but I don't know. I feel only that something is rising in me, saccharine sweet and bitter as gall in separate chunks, through my chest into my throat, pushing my head forward, forcing itself across my tongue, splattering somewhere. I'm disgusted with myself, I feel sullied from the inside, incurably transformed, and estranged. The common denominator for all three occurrences: the impossibility of seeing an end to this tormenting condition. Always the first time, no experience, no consolation. Unnerved, I stumble out every time to find my face still covered with tears as I walk down the street. Every time I decide to turn around and complain. No matter how fantastic the possibilities of the rekindling of feelings may be, that sort of thing doesn't belong in a museum, not even in a scientific institute. These are exaggerations distorting the truth and robbing us of our spontaneity in dealing with children.

39

Didn't go to the House today. I probably feared losing my self-control again in such a deplorable way. Instead, I went to a movie theater in town for the first time in a long time. I saw an old American movie, a story about teenagers, which didn't surprise me since once you're forced in a certain direction, you keep encountering the same problems. I would, of course, much have preferred to see a harmless love story, something from the dream factory, to get my mind off things. But I've got to admit that I was most pleasantly surprised. The kind of vague and absurd things that are conveyed to you in the House didn't show up here. Everything was plain, respectable adult psychology. A boy who's suffering from his father's self-right-eous lack of love develops a neurosis; after suffering a stroke, the father is clued in by the son's young girlfriend. He under-stands, stammers the thoroughly correct words indicating he approves of his son, and everything works out fine. After seeing this tidy work, I think the museum is behind the times. In the fi-nal analysis, a lot has happened to further the research of the role of childhood in our lives, and they have achieved results that simply can't be ignored.

40

Today I entered the House without fear, almost with slight con-descension. To my surprise, I was given an assignment this time. Standing at an open window, I had to press quite hard on my closed eyelids. (I might mention at this point that the tasks I was made to do were not yet assigned by individuals; there seemed to be no staff around or there was only one person of such unassuming demeanor that you forgot about him right away.) So here I was, pressing my fingers on my eyelids and not seeing a thing other than a reddish brightness, which was tra-versed by milky, wavy lines and in which individual black dots were bobbing around. As I increased or diminished the pres-sure, the images changed, above a brass-colored disk strange spiderwebs moved, in sudden darkness two little clouds floated by, delicate like velvet wings, from the edge to the center where they came together to form a dull, glistening star. Obsessed, I kept playing the game, which I obviously had practiced in my childhood, and after I had left the House, I tried it again. But it didn't work any longer, or something seemed to be missing now, namely that feeling of happiness which I had felt in there and which I can only term "bliss."

41

I keep catching myself making frequent use of the expression H.O.C. again, at least in my thoughts. The designation "House," which I've been using in this manuscript, is misleading. You think of a one-family home or a house in the country, on the order of Goethe's garden house, at any rate of something small, intimate, whereas the expanse of the museum is actually infinite. The contraction of the initial letters covers up the erroneous nature of the inscription, at which you never cease to wonder.

42

I've discovered something. There is something on the order of an information center in the H.O.C. after all. There are three attendants on hand to accompany you. You express your wish for this service by pressing a button, but you can't request a specific person. Besides, there are filmstrips that you can run yourself and which at any given time, as far as I can tell, show the events of a year, for example, 1901, 1905, 1910, 1920, so visitors apparently have an opportunity to identify relevant scenes from their childhood years. In addition, there is a lever that bears the somewhat puzzling inscription "Chronology"; once activated, it apparently serves the purpose of running off what is to be shown historically, that is, according to factual development. It wasn't until today that I discovered this lever, as well as the buttons with the years and the inscription "Attendants," on a kind of instrument panel near the front door, proof that the museum is still at the construction stage and that the management is trying to combat a certain initial impression of chaos. At first, I was a bit reluctant to activate these new gadgets. Finally, since the film buttons seemed the least intimidating, I pressed one of them. As a matter of fact, without much hesitation I chose the one that said 1905. On a little screen located next to the control panel, a street instantly appeared which was populated by lots of people but had only a few old-fashioned vehicles in it. A heavy streetcar on tracks was being pulled by a horse; the ladies, dressed in long, narrow skirts and walking with short, quick steps, wore enormous hats and kept their hands hidden in round fur muffs. The image disappeared, and you saw a cigar-shaped blimp which, dragged by soldiers, slowly crept out of a hangar. A man dressed in a white uniform and sporting an upturned, twisted mustache was standing on a platform surrounded by gentlemen in top hats and long frock coats. In a nightclub, couples swayed to a slow and sentimental tune. All of these scenes and the ones that followed were not shown in the manner of old movies, black and white, drab and jerky, but rather in colors true to nature and with authentic sound. You actually heard the dance music, the blaring of the military band, and the tired hoofbeat of the horse that was pulling the streetcar. You noticed that the ladies' high-button boots were brown and the banners black, white, and red, and you saw blue smoke rising from the men's cigars. Although the scenes had nothing objectionable about them at all, I experienced an intense dislike for the whole thing, the cause of which I can't explain.

43

Last night on my way home, the newspaper vendors shouted headlines that everyone knew meant a threat of war. Later that night, the same phrases were being written by planes in neon letters as is customary these days. I stopped, tilted my head back, and watched indifferently, almost obstinately, how the letters, which consisted of phosphorescent fog, originated and how the first word vanished almost before the last one was completed. Suddenly, it struck me that a threat of war these days meant an immediate threat of death and that no living thing would be exempt. It frightened me, but at the same time, I also saw the strange business that I've been occupied with these last weeks in a new light. My experiences in the H.O.C. were like the images that pass before the eyes of a dying person in rapid succession, and perhaps they had that same ultimate purpose. The fact that they would somehow not be entirely completed bothered me a great deal. I also thought at length about the fact that such a mass threat would have had to result in a mass visit to the museum, whereas this had not been the case at all. Finally, it occurred to me that the museum might have more than one entrance and that it was likely that a great many other people could be there at the same time without knowing about each other or ever seeing each other.

44

Attendant No. 2, who accompanied me today for the first time, is blind. I have to tell him what I see, and then he gives his explanations. Unfortunately, what I saw today was not too interesting. I saw a kind of peep-show stage, like a doll's house, only life-size. In the room, the walls of which were covered with dark-blue burlap, a floor lamp was on, whose base was made of alabaster and whose parchment shade was covered with glued-on photographs. At a round table, a man who was still young was playing chess with a child, a girl with long, flowing locks. A very beautiful young woman was sitting at the piano with her hands on the keys. A second girl was gluing small pictures apparently cut out of newspapers into an album on which old-fashioned flying machines could be seen. Underneath the piano, two other children were to be found, a fat little girl and a boy of about three, who were holding hands and seemed to be listening to something. The attendant explained that here my own family was portrayed. He added that my mother had played Chopin quite well, that my father had taught us to play chess when we were still quite young; also that my second-eldest sister had been crazy about flying after they had taken her to see the first flights of a young American at the so-called Bomstedt Field, a training center, and that my little brother and I had insisted on sitting under the piano while my mother was playing because we thought it sounded so much better there. I listened carefully, but I didn't really feel anything. In their horrible lifelessness, these oversize figures reminded me of the dressed-up mannequins that they place in a room when they want to simulate nuclear attacks and of whom there's nothing left after the explosion but a few scraps of material and a little dust.

45

Thought about the waiter. Another type that is almost extinct since all the better restaurants and coffeehouses in town have gone over to self-service. To be sure, to allow for the conservative taste of the public, these human automatons are usually somewhat disguised as waiter puppets in aprons and with napkins over their arms. However, neither the old-fashioned uniforms nor the stereotypical smiles of these automated waiters cover up the truth of the matter – the fact that only the outer shell is addressed and the guests are offered the meals they have ordered in a purely mechanical fashion. The waiter in this place is a human being who tends to the needs of another human being, and that, I think, is really extraordinary.

46

Was with Attendant No. 2 again. This time we entered a room

that appeared to be a laundry room, in which a gaslight was burning. Two young girls with flushed faces were pushing hot glowing rods into large, strangely shaped irons and guiding the irons over white linens while singing a song, in which they explained (highly illogically, as I'm just now noticing) that today there would be no ironing or sewing because it was His Majesty's birthday. Attendant No. 2, who apparently was a historian or sociologist by profession and only temporarily employed by the city, took the opportunity to give me a long lecture about the monarchy. The factual way in which he treated the theme really annoyed me. The monarchy of former times is distasteful to me, probably because it's part of my childhood, as it turns out now. Besides, I had the suspicion that all the experiences I've had in the company of the attendant may be strictly second rate.

47

The political tension that upset the city so much a couple of days ago has resolved itself again, but my apartment is beginning to seem unfamiliar to me. Actually, I only sleep there. When I go to the coffeehouse in the morning, I take my mail along, but in the last few days I haven't even opened my letters. They pile up on the table that the waiter reserves for me and on which I keep my books and manuscripts. As soon as I arrive, the waiter brings my breakfast and arranges my newspapers for me, lately he has even been marking in red certain articles that he thinks I might be interested in. Although he's very friendly, he upset me today by asking how much longer I thought I would be coming around. Since no one hardly ever comes to the coffee house, and since I'm not depriving anyone of a table, his question can only mean that he's planning to go on vacation or that the restaurant is going to close down because of lack of business. This thought bothers me since I can no longer imagine my visits to the House without stops at the coffeehouse before and after. I'm considering going over to the museum two or even three times a day instead of only once as I've been doing up until now. This way I would finish my studies more quickly without losing my pleasant haunt during this time.

48

I pushed the lever marked "Chronology." I figured that it really would start from the beginning, that is, with my birth. I would have been interested in seeing my mother's face when they presented me to her, me, her third daughter. (I once heard that she was terribly disappointed at the birth of my second-eldest sister; at mine, however, she's supposed to have been totally indifferent.) But I saw nothing of the kind. Instead, I had to get into a boat which to my surprise sailed across real water. The boat was packed. Adults and children with strange masklike faces were talking and laughing, but I didn't participate in their conversations. I was lying on my stomach on one of the narrow side benches dipping my hand in the water, which, warm and moldy black, swirled in eddies around my fingers. When I raised my head, I saw the shore that the boat was heading for, under the wide, bright sky high rushes and a wreath of autumnal, blazing forest. The touch of the water, now violent, now gentle, gave me a feeling of well-being as I experienced the attraction of a mysterious and enticing other world at the sight of the unfamiliar shore. On the whole, my mood was like the one last week when I was given the task of seeing all kinds of light images on the surface of my closed eyelids. A strange feeling of bliss, only this time it was awakened by the exterior world or an amazingly authentic replica of this exterior world.

49

If things continue with my visits to the H.O.C. the way they were yesterday and today, then I don't mind putting up with the fact that something is still wrong with the chronology and that you don't really learn anything rational and informative. I actually enjoy being there now, and I run over several times a day, not because I'm afraid they'll close down the coffeehouse but simply because I'm curious about the place. After being let in by Attendant No. 1, a quite ordinary custodian with an official cap, I find right behind the front door another exterior, but always a summery one, and because of this eternally beautiful summer alone, the visit is worth it. In addition, I recently had a sense of my own body, a pleasantly childlike body with bare arms and legs and thick, uncombed hair around my face. Yesterday I was running across a meadow, and the high, wet grasses brushed against my knees. I crawled in under the branches of an arborvitae or tree of life and stood there in the interior of the branches, in a darkish twilight that gave off an acrid and bitter smell. Finally, I climbed up the tree a bit and parted the branches. Around a circle of earth that had been dug up on the grass plot stood high and silent three more arborvitae, but on the circle of earth a white horse was being "lunged." Neither the boy, who was standing in the middle of the circle turning around and around with the long reins in his hands, nor the horse saw me, but when the white steed passed close by me once or twice, it threw back its head with a marvelous thrust. I had a feeling of security, and at the same time I experienced a powerful exhilaration brought about by the stomping and snorting of the horse, a feeling which like so many dreams is simply indescribable.

Note. The expression "to lunge," whose meaning has just become clear to me again, too, may not be familiar to the reader. It comes from the time when people still kept horses for riding and you exercised them on a long line called a lunge.

50

I've stopped thinking about the special effects of the museum. I don't care how the different sounds and smells are produced, and I don't even wonder any longer at the appearance of entire landscapes with natural sunlight, the fragrance of meadows, and the buzzing of mosquitoes. The plastic color films on the broad screen have produced the same kind of impression; the fact that you can now walk into such a landscape yourself may have its basis in a projection and sound technique that has escaped me so far. The layperson, and especially someone like me, for example, who sees little of physicists and technologists, can easily remain behind the times when it comes to these subjects. Left out of it for many decades because of a lack of foundation for any understanding of the actual world-shattering events of one's time, one calls technology to task while at the same time trusting it implicitly to perform even the most outrageous things.

51

Since there's never any way of getting hold of the museum administration, I attempted to repeat the boat trip today through sheer determination. I had no luck, but I did have two experiences that were similar to the first one. I am walking, as if through a forest, through a thicket of finely feathered plants, which I *know* only reach up to the hips of an adult. Outside a little train is passing by, puffing and whistling; as soon as the tones slowly fade away, it is completely quiet. On the fleshy stalks of the asparagus ferns, tiny snails are sitting in their little houses, caterpillars twist and stretch their grass-green bodies, at my feet is a dead mole with its pale little hands stretched out in front of it. Black beetles with shiny backshields stagger back and forth, above the pale-green lilac tops a dragonfly hovers while drawing its magic circle. I walk very slowly as if through an enchanted forest, Potnia Theron, Mistress of All Creatures – which I hate to touch and which I feel superior to for some inexplicable reason, in the same way that an older child feels superior to younger children.

At my second visit to the House, I was sitting in the grass in the hot July sun. I picked one stem after the other from the dandelions that grew around me, removing the yellow heads and forming the stems, which were full of a white, gooey milk, into a ring by pushing the thinner ends into the fatter ones. Pinching off the yellow blooms with my nails and squeezing out the milk was enjoyable, but putting the wreath together was even more enjoyable, because something that hadn't been there before was created, namely a chain that got longer and longer. Again, a feeling of secret power that carried me as if on wings.

52

The organization of the museum still leaves something to be desired. There are days when I experience things very different from the scenes that I have just described, and those experiences are like the chapters in a beautiful book of memoirs. The feeling of being haunted by something piecemeal, like by a sweetish, sickening smell or a scratchy moaning sound recurring at intervals, is pure torture, especially when an environment that is part of it refuses to make itself visible even with the utmost patience. The tasks that are required of me (lately by Attendant No. 1, the custodian) I find particularly foolish, like yesterday, for example, when I was forced to move a green-printed curtain secured with brass rings back and forth on a brass rod, perhaps a hundred times. No physical feeling, no glimpse into the interior of the piece of furniture (maybe a low toy closet) in front of which the curtain was placed. Only the slight rattle with which the rings hit each other, only the suggestion of musty-smelling cloth. Another experience of this sort was more pleasant: close before my eyes in a mahogany box, a steel cylinder with pinlike protuberances was turning slowly, whereby the long, soft teeth of a steel cog swept across the uneven surface. The touch generated a fine, rippling music which sometimes came to a halt and then started up again, as if ethereally light dancers were hovering in the air for a moment, only to turn again with graceful movements.

53

Again something very beautiful which, it seems to me during the instruction, is "fabricated" by none other than the adults, who thereby come into new focus, that of magic. A dark room, whispering, lots of children sitting on the rug, the smell of sulfur; on a tiny stage in the background a forest ravine above which yellow lightning is flashing and on which Samuel, the evil spirit, appears, conjured up by my mother's strangely transformed voice. Immediately afterward, in the same area, something quite different, a star projected on a spread-out sheet whose colorful individual parts explode again and again to give way to new, marvelously pure and shiny configurations. In the afternoon, again the magical power of the grownups, this time my father dipping his finger in the waterglass for a moment and tracing the edge of the glass, then the fine edges of several half-filled wine glasses, thereby producing gentle music, alternately soft and loud, but ever fleeting.

54

Because the first violent snowstorms of the season started yesterday just as I was about to leave, the waiter offered me lodging for the night. Some rooms, he said, were available to guests passing through. I wondered why I had never seen anything of these overnight guests before, but I followed the waiter anyway to an upper story where he opened the door to a room that looked like a simple, old-fashioned hotel room. Instead of a couch, there was a genuine, large bed of dark wood, and from the half-open window long white curtains billowed into the narrow room. There was no lamp on the nightstand, but when I had lain down and turned out the light, the broad beam of light from a window across the courtyard shone into my room. It was a good feeling not to go to sleep right away. I pulled the sheet up over my head, at first to protect myself from the snowy wind, then out of pure delight. Then suddenly there was a dimly lit cave around me, a tent in which my limbs stretched out and relaxed again until I found a position that I hadn't slept in for years, that of an embryo in the womb. Suddenly I was a child at play, the tent was my castle, my fingers moved around in it like servants doing my bidding. Later, I put a crumpled corner of the sheet to my mouth, pressing my lips against the warm bed linens and intensely sucking them, while cupping my bare knee with my hand in pure rapture. When I woke up the next morning, it seemed as if I had been over there in the House again during the night, and for the first time I had the suspicion that the coffeehouse belonged less to the outside world than to this House, indeed, that it itself was a part of this strange institution. It wasn't until I had washed myself with ice-cold water from the rose-flowered wash basin that I realized I must have been dreaming and that this room really was nothing more than a pretty ordinary, you might almost say kind of run-down, hotel room.

55

My activities for the newspapers have almost come to a complete stop. I can afford it because I'm just a free-lance contributor, and, besides, the waiter lets me charge all my meals until I can pay for them (out of the proceeds for the account I'm writing now). I don't do a whole lot of reading anymore either, just the morning papers and now and then something in one of the many newspapers that the coffeehouse takes (for whom, I wonder?) The waiter still marks this or that article in red; for example, just recently a piece on the nature of people born in the different signs of the zodiac. Whereas many of the astrological types treated there by the author seem to be depicted in rather unkind terms, he's quite easy on the ones born in Aquarius (my sign). They are unstable and unpredictable, frequently an enigma to their friends, but imaginative and receptive to anything new. Although I know that horoscopes of that sort are pure humbug without any knowledge of the person involved, I did make a note of one comment that had to do with the self-sufficiency, the ability to be alone, of those who are born in Aquarius. In fact, now that I think of it, I was alone in almost all the scenes I viewed in the H.O.C., and I was quite happy with this solitary state. On the other hand, I've found my later life truly worth living only when I loved another person and he returned my love. The egocentricity of my present endeavor really makes me unhappy, no matter how enjoyable the visits to the museum may have been. How long has it been since I last saw Carl — and we used to be together almost daily! To think that I've not even bought him a Christmas present.

56

I must confess that the things I've been shown do appear in a certain order after all. Child in the garden, child in front of the toy closet, and so on. Today I was sitting in a streetcar (apparently the horse-drawn one copied from the 1905 film), that is, I was kneeling on the seat and looking out the window. The streetcar rumbled through the main street of a small town, past a lot of shops. On the shop signs there were large, often colorful letters that I was trying to recognize and sound out in a loud voice. The delight I experienced when the symbols spelled out a familiar word was immense, as if I had created all those words myself and along with them the designated objects, or as if at this moment I had made them unforgettably my own.

57

I've forgotten to report that I recently had them show me another film. Without further ado, a big ocean liner in heavy seas appeared on the screen, emerging from the fog between high waves only to disappear again. A graphic presentation of icebergs followed, that is, I saw drawings of several pyramid-shaped formations jutting up with a little point over a horizontal wavy line, presumably the ocean surface. Thereupon many isolated scenes on the steamship itself, which probably was about to sink, people holding on to each other, falling on their knees and praying, or madly going through their suitcases. The whole thing didn't seem to be very characteristic of one specific incident since shipwrecks unfortunately occur all the time, and the only way you could figure out that these scenes took place in the past was from the old-fashioned clothing of the passengers. Finally, after being forced to watch one of the shipwrecked strangle another person in the water, you could see only a piece of the white liner jutting out of the waves, the bow on which the word TITANIC was written, apparently the name of the ship.

58

I've moved into the little room on the upper floor of the coffeehouse, partly to save myself the long walk in bad weather, but most of all because the recent pre-Christmas magic of the stores is getting on my nerves. In all the display windows, and on streets and squares all over town as well, you can already see lighted Christmas trees, that is to say, trees with continuously blinking electric lights, which are merely supposed to entice the consumer to spend. The daily sight of these things finally makes you long for Christmas to be over so that all that gaudiness will disappear again to make room for the cold and invigorating soberness of the new year. Aside from this lack of interest and a certain fatigue, which results from all museum visits, I don't feel the least bit unsocial or depressed. On the contrary, I feel like getting in touch with my friends again and especially with those who, like me at one time, didn't like to think about their childhoods. Once in a while, I go out fully intending to pay someone a visit; quite happy and eager to leave, I hurry to the end of the cul-de-sac. I resolve to tell everybody about the H.O.C., how much fun it is to be there, and how, guided by a wise management, you gradually lose whatever fear and reluctance you may have had. The fact that I turn around again after all, even before I have reached the main street, has its own rationale: I can't predict the consequences of this kind of sharing; even in the fairy tales the tattletales were somehow severely punished. Besides, I'm superstitious and don't trust this peaceful lull; from time to time, even at this very moment, I have the feeling that if I didn't exercise the greatest caution, something terrible might happen to me in the House.

59

My unpleasant premonition last night has not been confirmed, at least not as far as I myself am concerned. Today I was leaning out a window, actually one of these oval apertures that you find in historic buildings from the Baroque era. What I saw down there was a broad, level, sandy square on which soldiers in colorful uniforms were lined up or marching around, as an officer with drawn sword rode ahead or a standard-bearer walked in front. The sun was blazing, and right below my window a soldier, tall as a chimney, suddenly fell over and lay stiff as a board with staring, open eyes in his white face. I was convinced he was dead, and I was upset that no one carried him away or did anything about it. I screamed and waved my hands, but was held back. Suddenly Attendant No. 2 was at my side although I hadn't even called, in fact, had completely forgotten about his existence. What's all this? I asked angrily as the soldiers kept marching outside, raising and lowering their legs like mechanical dolls. The attendant called the event a parade; he explained that the strange window was part of the royal stables, that the fine music that could be heard in the distance came from a historical glockenspiel, and that the commander in chief, Germany's last emperor, Wilhelm II, was present. I was ready to believe everything he said, only my own presence there seemed highly unlikely. Next chance they get, they'll probably show me the emperor Napoleon in Versailles and insist I was present at the coronation.

60

I still haven't gotten together with Carl, but I finally did get him a Christmas present. It's kind of childish and not worth a whole lot, but I'm happy with it. I couldn't get it through a store and, in fact, acquired it only by sheer chance. The waiter, who was in the process of cleaning up, passed by my table yesterday carrying a long, narrow cardboard box. The box contained, as he told me, a little remnant of some sparklers, only not the usual short ones that you put on your Christmas tree, but yard-long ones that give you half an hour's worth of incredibly colorful fireworks. At my request, the waiter parted with two of these rather plain-looking but very promising sticks in gray wrappings, and now I'm looking forward even more to celebrating Christmas with Carl, who gets a special kick out of such childish pleasures. By then I hope I'll be done with my studies in the museum, provided, of course, that I continue to go there faithfully and don't let myself be detained by anyone.

61

I have the impression that horses, these animals that unfortunately are almost extinct now, play an important role in the H.O.C. You frequently get a whiff of stables, also the smell of saddles and leather balm, with which certain creaking and rocking noises are associated. A little while back, the pungent smell of insect repellent was produced so accurately that all the possible feelings of summer, like the rolling of wheels, the breathing of dust, the coolness of shade, were evoked so authentically that you had the sensation of riding in a carriage in spring. The experience I had today, however, took place on a different and much more sinister plane. The place was a deserted asphalt street, part of the road I used to take to school, as was evident from the satchel strapped to my back. I was trotting down the long street while rattling a little stick, which I had picked up, across the iron fence rails in the front gardens. This sound was suddenly drowned out by close, thundering hoofbeats. I looked around me and saw a team of enormous, coal-black horses coming straight toward me, apparently without a driver. Scared to death, I rushed to the other side of the street. Then when I noticed the pursuers, stomping and neighing, headed in that direction, too, I rushed back and forth again in a horrible zigzagging. The moment I saw the rearing heads of the horses and the flashing horseshoes of their front hoofs right above me, I was dismissed from the museum, found myself outside again, on the other side of the entrance but shaking all over and covered with perspiration. The purpose of all this unnecessary torture, I take it, has no basis in actual fact but is merely some childhood dream. Nevertheless, the fear is still with me, and I have the feeling that this dream persecution is only the beginning of other even more unpleasant experiences.

62

No dreams today but instead other equally loathsome things. I'm wondering if I did something wrong. Maybe I've offended the museum management by ignoring certain regulations. There's been a kind of anteroom lately, with sea-green carpeting and roughly plastered walls. As I waited there a little while back, I saw figures, landscapes, and profiles in the plaster, an entire little world that I liked but immediately forgot about as I went on. It may just be that directions are contained there in letters, numbers, or entire sentences which I have overlooked to my detriment. Maybe they also noticed with displeasure that I made so little use of the contraption with historical films and that I, for the most part, chose not to take advantage of the attendants' company. At any rate, the mood in the H.O.C. has changed. They're not well-disposed toward me anymore. The reader of this account will immediately understand what I mean by that, when I outline very briefly what I was made to do during my three visits today. During my first visit early this morning, I lay stretched out in a pleasantly airy cloud-shape above the treetops of an old garden, looking through the branches down into the green dawn. At the same time, however, I was also down below, a fat little girl, peeling tender, white strips of bark off the trunk of a young birch tree, when a man suddenly came toward me, the gardener with his hoe, red-haired, angry, clearly the enemy. In either of my guises I didn't understand one word of what he was saying. I only saw him coming closer, yelling something, his coal-black pregnant dog keeping close to his side. During my second visit, it was night. I was standing barefoot by the window in the nursery, eager to see the moon and the man in the moon. But the bright disk was covered with clouds, and in the courtyard below my window, naked, long-tailed creatures crept from the stables toward a puddle that had formed underneath the water pump, a disgusting pack which finally dispersed, frightened by the closing of a door, only to disappear with wild, lurching movements. During my third visit, nothing at all happened, and yet this was the most frightening of them all. Again nighttime, a different nursery (by the way, much more faded, so probably it was longer ago), shadowy bedsteads, the breathing of my sisters, only I was awake. A clock ticks and strikes, ticks and strikes, ticks and strikes, and with every quarter hour I'm pulled further away into a midnightlike realm far away, which for children is full of the most frightful dangers. On the nightstand there's a bell that I'm not allowed to touch, but my hand nevertheless reaches out for it again and again until I grab it after all in the despair of my loneliness and shake it, wildly, madly, until my sisters and brother wake up and start crying, until I hear footsteps on the stairs, the footsteps . . .

63

I thought a lot about the aforementioned footsteps today. I can still hear them, they are light and yet tired, as if they belonged to someone who was making numerous trips through the house every day, up the stairs and down the stairs. They are not my mother's footsteps, which (at least, as I remember them from her later years) would have been energetic, rested, and fresh. The footsteps, however, that saved me from my fear of death in the H.O.C., so difficult to understand now, are dragging and yet full of infinite willingness to help. They are, simply, the footsteps of consolation. The fact that I can't connect them with any person or any face bothers me a great deal.

64

It seems utterly strange to me now that I once thought the House of Childhood might represent something like a sanatorium, an institution for the treatment of already existing or threatening neuroses, for example during menopause or other periods of crisis, when actually it's a totally unhealthy place, as I'm seeing more and more clearly. In this connection, I might mention certain physical states that I've been subjected to in the H.O.C. during the last few days, for example, the swelling of individual limbs or even of the whole body to an elephantine size and weight and the subsequent sudden shrinking to the dryness of a grasshopper and the weight of a fly. My fear of being stuck in one of these states is tremendous every time, I feel I'm in danger of losing my normal shape and along with that my self. Although this morbid imagination usually disappears very quickly, I nevertheless have been feeling worse since my last visits to the museum than I did previously. Although I'm living exclusively in the coffeehouse now and go to bed very early, I don't sleep well at all and am pale and exhausted the next morning. If it weren't entirely against my grain not to complete things that I've made up my mind to carry out, I would forget about any further visits to the museum for health reasons. When I leave the H.O.C., I'm sometimes tempted to walk right past the coffeehouse and simply continue on home. But that, too, takes a certain determination that I may not be able to summon until I've had more pleasant experiences in the H.O.C.

65

Things aren't getting any better, in fact, they're getting worse with every day that passes. To the feeling of fear, which the museum management is trying so ingeniously to transmit, a new, unpleasant feeling has been added, namely disgust with myself. Sure, I'm the same timid, agreeable child that I was in the last remedial courses. I cry a lot (yesterday a whole lesson's worth) for no apparent reason and with curious enjoyment. But in addition to that, I'm still something else, a cauldron of sudden anger that begins to bubble and boil and spill over just like that, a puppet that can be made to stamp her feet, hammer with her fists, and pull a stranger's hair as I did in the H.O.C., only to run away and hide, fearful of myself and, lately, of this brand-new feeling, of shame.

66

Again, the same dissatisfaction, the same despair, but for a totally different and not so simple reason, a complex occurrence during which, as has been happening lately, different scenes change rapidly one after the other and then merge. Along these lines, I saw today in rapid succession, as on a revolving stage, an Oriental room – that is, a room furnished with heavy drapes, carpets, and round brass trays – an arbor, and a figure walking very upright down the narrow street, oddly dressed, with a severe brown face. Right afterward, I found myself behind the arbor. Two little girls, also of foreign extraction, were sitting next to me on a wooden board; along the wooden partition stood my brother, completely naked. Smiling innocently, he was playing with a beanstalk. I myself have put him there to show my friends how he's different, but the way they look at him now, at this beautiful little Sebastian, with their curious, piercing eyes, makes me sick to my stomach. The revolving stage keeps turning: the room again, then the exotic old woman with her staring eyes, then the wooden partition with the red-flowering beanstalks and the naked boy, until all of a sudden everything disappears and Attendant No. 3 is standing before me in a white coat. New neighbors, he says, from far away, the attraction of the exotic, the exposure of a loved one out of the need for approval, sexual curiosity, and so on; as always, he speaks in captions, and I'm not sure what to make of them.

67

The instructional methods used in the museum are getting more and more obscure since there is now, in addition to the remedial courses where you feel you revert to a childish state, in addition to the films and lectures, something on the order of a properties course. During these sessions, you remain "an adult" after entering the museum, and the instruction takes place in very neutral rooms equipped with closets and shelves full of teaching tools: a drawer is opened every time, and the desired items are brought to you by the attendant. Today the custodian first of all showed me a rack of children's clothes, most of which were made by the same unskilled hand and in pretty much the same style, shifts with smocking, pink calico dresses with three flounces adorned with Valencia lace. But there were also sailor's outfits with wide collars and bows and anchors embroidered in gold, and then there was a black velvet smock with an Irish lace collar which, as the custodian informed me, had belonged to my brother. The second closet was opened for me by Attendant No. 3, to my surprise. He took out a doll, a male doll actually, with peeling facial skin, frayed pants, and a torn jacket, and reported with almost mock seriousness that it was this one I had dragged around with me all the time and had been especially fond of, whereas I had disliked the dressing and undressing, putting to bed, caring for and mothering of girl dolls.

68

I don't care for Attendant No. 3, especially since he keeps showing up without being asked, contrary to the regulations. In the suggestion box that I'm thinking of placing in the museum, since there apparently isn't one, I'm going to lodge a complaint about his supercilious behavior and his method of labeling things and then disappearing, pleased with himself and acting as if something had already been set in motion. Another item that I would find fault with is the senseless exaggeration that the museum is guilty of. When I pass a garden full of crazy people (again on my way to school), it's highly unlikely that in reality we're talking about more than one or at the most two lunatics. There's no way that there would be a man every couple of feet who would either utter bleating sounds or let his limbs dangle oddly or stick his head through the iron fence rails with an insane grin, as they showed me today. And it's just as unlikely that my big sisters would have fought the way they just showed me, I mean, so full of passion and anger that I slipped into bed and under the covers for fear of something incredibly bad happening. All siblings fight, every child comes into contact with abnormal persons sooner or later. But where would we be if we were to dramatize things to such an extent and treat them in this solemn way? Also, my experiences today only prove that I'm to be tortured in the museum and punished for something, perhaps for my initial stubborn resistance. But these practices only bring out a healthy spirit of contradiction in me. It can't have been that way. Not that horrible.

69

And yet, that's how it was. Nothing is directed at me person-
ally, nothing concerns me alone. Or have you, dear reader of
these pages, never walked down a dark passage and peeked
through a door standing ajar only to find inside the room someone (an adult) who sat and cried? And didn't you want to run
up and throw your arms around that person, and yet you
stayed where you were for the longest time with your heart in
your throat? Why? Because that sort of thing simply mustn't be
true, because grownups were supposed to be strong, because
they, least of all, were allowed to feel fear and pain like you.
And didn't you finally go away, far away, and hold your ears to
shield yourself from this impropriety that you couldn't forget —
ever again?

Note. The custodian told me that in my own case it was a
matter of a nanny who was being replaced by an educated gov-
erness and who had been asked to vacate her room next to the
nursery. I keep trying in vain to remember the girl's face. I know
only one thing: the footsteps on the stairs were hers . . .

70

I long for the days when I didn't need any explanations during
my visits to the museum. The attendants, even the uneducated
custodian, tend to intellectualize everything, which sometimes
makes me wonder whether there's any hanky-panky going on,
although you would have to make allowances for the fact that
this is a research institute. Besides, the consolation of a rational
explanation is usually totally ineffective since you're transformed in a clever way and have no access to the rational in the
H.O.C. Even long after I've left the museum, I'm under the spell
of what I've just experienced. Today, for example, there was a
park path at dusk, from which I looked up in the sky (guided by

a hand), when a horrible dizziness suddenly seized hold of me as if I were standing at the edge of a precipice. For the first time in my life, the sky was transparent, an accumulation of air, a terrible emptiness that knew no bounds. On the way out, everything was different, the arched ceiling finite, a great hall of angels, a platform for the throne of the good Lord. Even now this image sneaks in again and again only to be crushed, dissolved, destroyed forever. So that I wouldn't have to look upward any longer, I yanked the plump, white berries, the ones that sound so funny when you step on them, off the shrubs by the roadside. In the puddles at my feet I saw the same sky, there was no getting away from it. I had a feeling of terrible abandonment, from which neither the indistinct grownup next to me nor the windows being illuminated here and there could protect me. I was desperate, and to tell the truth, I still am. It didn't do the least bit of good for Attendant No. 3 to explain that I was coming home from a geography class at the time and that it was my teacher who through his routine, scientific explanation had destroyed my image of the universe.

71

Real winter weather of the kind you often hear old people talk about. The snow is even staying in the city, and especially in our cul-de-sac, where there's little traffic, you feel removed to a primitive place in the mountains. Today the waiter had to shovel the way to the museum for me, which he did with great facility in spite of his age. But my fear of being snowed in at the H.O.C. was great. A couple of times I've asked the waiter to go out in the street around noon to check the weather. The snowflakes, which keep falling with no pause, are quite unusually large and thick, almost like chunks of white bread or like wads of cotton, dry and heavy. Although the waiter has promised not to leave me in the lurch, I'm filled with anxiety every time he goes out. The thought of spending even one day being exposed to the ceaseless torture of the museum seems horrible, and I'm afraid that the waiter finally will not be able to deal with the masses of snow. I would then, circumstances permitting, be compelled to ask to stay in the museum overnight and, once established, perhaps have to remain there out of sheer laziness, the same way I ended up staying at the coffee house. To begin with, nobody would come looking for me there since I've broken off all ties to the outside world for the time being, but later on any trace of me would be completely gone; even the police wouldn't find me.

72

The panicky state I've gotten myself into stems more than anything from the appearance of a certain Herr Leisegang or Liesegang that I've run into several times in the H.O.C. in the last few days. He's a skinny, hollow-cheeked little man with inflamed eyes and a sty on his lower left eyelid. The custodian explained that this man had owed my parents quite a bit of money, that they had never pushed for payment, but that he kept coming around asking for new loans. I've met him on the stairs of my parents' house, in the hall, and in front of the door to my mother's room, and every time he wrings his hands and cries. His outward appearance is really repulsive, and I can't figure out for the life of me why he would turn to me, a child, with his pleas. Since I don't seem to be able to get a satisfactory explanation out of the custodian, I turned to Attendant No. 2. As is his wont, he gave me a long lecture about the expression "bankrupt" and what it meant as well as about capitalism in terms of economics, the credit system, etc. Out of all this, only the word "misery" made an impression on me. I imagined a kind of swamp or mudhole which, once you had gotten into it, there was no way of getting out of, and I seemed to notice that little Herr Leisegang smelled of swamp and left wet tracks. I was afraid that he would grab me and pull me down with him, and when he actually did take me by the hand one day in the street, I ran away upset and out of breath but at the same time full of disgust with myself. I'm still suffering from this disgust with my own cowardice. Besides, I'm aware that I still have the greatest trouble imagining the explanations of Attendant No. 2. They are part of a world out there which is growing paler and paler whereas everything that happens in the H.O.C. is gaining in meaning. I can't imagine how I was totally capable of settling my affairs with a certain sharpness of mind just a little while back. It's a good thing I took care of things in advance and that I don't have to bother about making business decisions in my present condition.

73

Sometimes the House of Childhood seems to me like a mountain that I'm descending into, deeper and deeper to the heart of the earth. In the interior of the earth there are terrible caverns and tunnels without exits where firedamp threatens, but there are also gold and silver veins, precious stones, and semi-precious stones, as I imagine them down there, I mean, already polished and sparkling beautifully. I sometimes feel as if I were reaching the nucleus of the earth as I sink deeper and deeper, a chamber of gleaming light. I remember a poem – "the heart of the earth doth a glow exude, je suis là bas, béatitude" – as you can see, an impossible rhyme, which I must have thought up as a result of early language training. (I've continued the habit of dreaming up such little sayings of comfort and edification and reciting them to myself in bed in the evening, but, of course, I'll never share these with anyone.) To pursue such lines of thought and to abandon oneself to them is relaxing. Your fear disappears, and the old attraction of the museum is reestablished in an instant. Besides, since a thaw has suddenly set in and I don't have to fear being held in the H.O.C. against my will, I set out with greater peace of mind. Today's "precious stone": a pale-green sparkling of leaves; in addition, the fragrance of an alder tree and the countless, distant calls of a cuckoo would have been pure joy if it hadn't been for the accompanying painful feeling of having lost my native home, probably as a result of the experience I had just been through.

74

The noon and evening meals they come up with in the coffee-house are light and good. As for the selections themselves, which I leave entirely to the waiter, he has erred on only one occasion, when he brought me roasted chestnuts from an Italian vendor who was roaming the streets with his oven. Although I've acquired a fondness for these over the last few years, I experienced an intense dislike for them after the first few bites. The very same thing happened to me with the spinach that they fixed in the coffeehouse. On the other hand, the strangely childish foods the waiter has been serving lately (rice porridge with cinnamon, semolina pudding, and that sort of thing) taste especially good to me, and today I was just as thrilled about a concoction of mashed potatoes and applesauce, which ordinarily would taste quite bland. Since they have run out of cigarettes in the coffeehouse, and the waiter seems to have a hard time getting a new supply, I've given up smoking, a decision which, by the way, cost me almost no effort at all.

75

Nothing about "precious stones," nothing further about secret bliss. Instead, a series of very banal experiences which, however, portrayed in the usual dramatic way they have in the H.O.C., took on the nature of catastrophes. The worst thing today: I was standing on a wooden platform with wet cotton fabric clinging to my body, around me a group of children with ghostly pale faces and purple lips, among them a heavy-set man. One after the other, the children put on a heavy, cold belt with a slack-hanging rope attached to it, which the fat man was holding on to. Shivering all over and with chattering teeth, the children stepped out on a high board that extended out over the black surface of the water, and at the command of the man they let themselves drop into the deep from its slightly teetering end. And now it was my turn. I didn't want to put on that belt, and as they forced it over me anyway, I held on to the wooden balustrade and then started hitting the fat man with both fists on his oily, hairy chest. Tearing himself away from me, the fat man pushed me into the water backward, not from the diving board but from the platform where we were standing. Grayish green whirlpools surrounded me, then air again, then the other again, that horrible something that makes you suffocate. Over there someone was pulling the line, slackening it, and pulling it again, finally I was hauled back to the steps. After that (but here, too, the sequence was not executed in order) I sat hiding on the steps to a bathing cabin wanting to die so that I wouldn't have to go through this again – this smell of the damp mats and wet, cold human skin, the sergeant's voice constantly bellowing in the din, this tiny piece of sky that the swallows soar through so wonderfully light and carefree.

76

The new invention by means of which you can send promotional materials around town via tiny airplanes operated by remote control is being widely used by the big department stores in town. Even our cul-de-sac, which certainly doesn't constitute a very lucrative market outlet, receives this service from none other than the large department store on the corner of the main street. In quite leisurely fashion, these little Santa Clauses, Christmas angels, and other figures buzz by the windows of the upper stories, turning around at the end of the street and flying back again. One of these planes broke down today, going into a spin and landing on the sidewalk where the waiter picked it up and brought it in for me to have a closer look at. What was attached to the tiny engine between the wings was a kind of Christmas tree, but one without branches and pine needles, made entirely of white flakes and silvery tinsel, enthroned on a folded, golden sleeve that flared out and was covered with small, pink candles. The waiter placed this attractive creation in front of the mirror on the mantle, whereupon it immediately appeared in every corner, that is, in the many other mirrors of the old-fashioned furnished room. He promised to light the little candles on Christmas Eve, and apparently he has also prepared a surprise for me for that occasion. I don't dare admit to him that I'm not counting on spending Christmas Eve here at all but at home with Carl. After all, it's only the eighteenth of December today, and a lot of unexpected things may come up in the meantime.

77

Thought about my last experiences in the H.O.C. and especially about the swimming incident. A death wish, at the age of six or eight – I guess that's another one of these exaggerations that the museum constantly is guilty of. Still, I couldn't find peace of mind when I thought about it today. I had to take to the streets, but I didn't walk in the usual direction but rather to the exit of the cul-de-sac. I wanted to see children, hear voices, read their faces, to find out if there really was such a thing as the kind of despair you don't share with anyone, these silent tragedies that no adult ever suspects. If things were really the way they led you to believe in the H.O.C., these experiences would take on a totally different meaning: the things they showed you there were intended to open the eyes of adults. After their apprenticeship they were supposed to understand children better. There was something liberating about this thought, I was beginning to think that my task was almost done, I was already playing with the thought of returning to my apartment and my former activities. But unfortunately the experiences I had in that short distance to the main street weren't at all what I had expected. I saw a couple of children playing around a puddle, and their eyes were beaming with excitement and happiness. A little girl who was staring longingly at a doll in a store window was filled with boundless confidence that she would indeed get that doll for Christmas. Finally, I ran into two boys who were busily tearing rails off a fence and who seemed to derive the greatest pleasure from doing so. Subdued, I returned to the coffeehouse. I still don't know if it's just that I keep looking at the children out there with the terribly oblivious eyes of an adult, or if maybe I myself was a special case, an overly sensitive, whimpering creature. I know only one thing: I've got to get over there again . . .

78

Was at the House quite early this morning. The custodian led me up a steep staircase into a dimly lit attic where dust particles danced in a shaft of light from a dormer window. He left me alone, and I immediately started going through a box in which props and spare parts for the puppet theater were stored. A stack of books was lying next to it. I interrupted what I was doing and opened up one book and another to read the titles. One book was called *The Birth of a Man*. I opened it up, and, sure enough, it described a birth. I read on in the strangest way, seizing hold of the words, as I might pull plants out of the soil, roots and all. Then they themselves turned into what was being described: forceps, blood, water, umbilical cord, and afterbirth; screams sounded in my ears, and a sickening odor spread, permeating the dusty and stuffy air of the enclosed room. My fear was so great that when the custodian handed me a note, as I was leaving the attic, I was in no condition to read what it said, and again much later, when I went back to the coffeehouse, I tried in vain to establish a connection between what I had just gone through and my later experiences. I mean by that the births of my own children: whereas these latter were clear as day in my mind, that former experience remained horrible and dark, a fear that I couldn't conquer. I don't have the note anymore – all the items you get in the H.O.C. eventually disappear mysteriously. I only remember that under the heading, "Attendant No. 3," it had the words "Maxim Gorky, sexual curiosity, shock." I'm happy to know the author of the book since I'll now be able to read the relevant pages sometime and test their authenticity. Also, the explanations of Attendant No. 3 are clear for once, albeit unnecessary, since my fear of the secret reading is still with me.

79

The film that I just ran, more out of concern for not aggravating the museum management by disregarding their expensive equipment than out of any real need, surprised me. One is, after all, inclined to regard the decades before the First World War as a kind of golden era, a long-lasting period of peace, affluence, and generally good times. The damp, ugly basements, the dreary gray factories, the deplorable rear courtyards, and the awful refuse dumps that just appeared on the screen from none other than the year 1910 didn't correspond to this idea at all. The camera angle was very clever, as if the objects had been filmed from the window of a local train passing through the tenements of a metropolis, flying past, then coming to rest again and focusing on details – a consumptive girl at a sewing machine, children rummaging through the trash, a man staggering out of a tavern with an empty pay envelope in his hand, a shabby bedroom with a pale woman in the bed. A kind of didactic film, not all that glitters is gold, dragoon helmets and proletarian caps, bourgeois decency and the misery of the worker – all of it rather depressing and in no way likely to affirm or even increase my faith in the historical era that my childhood falls in.

80

Thought again about the methods used in the museum, that is, about the selections made from the archive of memories. Why are these films (which are surely being shown to me only) this way and not that? Why do I have to go through these and not other personal experiences again? I must admit that I'm not happy with the selections, that if I'd had any idea at all as to what was available in the museum, I was hoping to find very different, more informative material. The truly personal experiences aren't there, as far as I'm concerned, nor are there any really clear explanations of the apparent gloom of my childhood from a certain point in time on. No matter how shaken I am every time I leave the House, the things I've experienced there nevertheless seem extremely ordinary and inconsequential when I look at them from the distance, for example after a good evening meal. Any dramatic touches are totally lacking.

How differently literature has been able to explain and portray the loneliness and pain of children. In fact, so has modern film. I remember a movie in which a little girl holding her mother's hand is standing in front of the window of a travel agency looking enraptured at a white ship displayed there and then seeing a stranger in the mirror of the glass pane and her mother's face, smiling encouragingly at this man, whereupon everything falls apart: her close relationship with her mother, her trust, her happiness. You might also think of Hanno Buddenbrook as he walks up the stairs with his father while the lieutenant is visiting his mother – these are concrete examples that readily substantiate our existential anxiety. The fact that the same things don't happen in my case, that I'm not in charge of this quite ordinary child's life after being transformed daily by means of these artificial presentations in the museum, fills me with mistrust. For some mysterious reason, I always assume that something crucial is being kept from me.

81

The big red table covered with green oilcloth under the gas lamp in the nursery was turned upside down, its legs wrapped in thin wicker. Kitchen chairs and little rattan seats were piled on top of it, stalks jutted out here and there, masts with flags. I was sitting on a stack of garden cushions, my arms around my little brother, sailing with him across distant oceans toward strange shores. The wardrobe is Mount Rogo, the four little white beds are the meadows of the Milky Way, through the division between the drapes the single glowering eye of the Great Bear is looking in. In the perilous wilderness, my brother is singing in his bright silvery voice. How I hold on to him, tenderly, fearfully, as if all this could suddenly come to an end. Just as in the H.O.C., where both – the feeling of remaining imprisoned in a childlike state and the fear of growing up – always exist side by side.

82

It keeps happening over and over again that isolated, rather uninteresting things are shown to the museum visitor for hours on end and with the most detailed explanations, whereas the most beautiful landscapes appear only fleetingly like a mirage and without any closer description. Today they bored me by putting a strange object, a kind of leg splint made of metal and leather in my hand, they made me turn it back and forth and examine it from every angle. The custodian pointed out how well made the object was and what fine, durable metal had been used. He didn't let up until I had touched with my fingers the gleaming metal rods, the well-formed joints, and the smooth brown exterior of the legging, and several times he called my attention to the fact that the inside of the foot support, the insole, was lined with the most delicate pink leather. Finally I myself had to put on the splint, which apparently served to correct bone deformities, maybe even an ordinary fallen arch, and walk around with it on, whereby, I must confess, a slight creaking of the metal joints suddenly caused a most unpleasant sensation in me that had nothing whatsoever to do with the objective examination of this orthopedic contraption.

83

A new frightening contrivance, is now at the disposal of visitors to the museum – incidentally without their consent and even against their will – which enables them to see themselves not as in a mirror, but totally from the outside. The transformation occurs quite suddenly without prior warning, and for that reason there's something really terrifying about it. It was twice as unpleasant for me today, because the self-portrait I was shown bore no resemblance to what I had imagined. When I stepped into the House, they had put the splint on me again to my dismay. The door that the custodian opened for me led to a playground, which I entered with a certain curiosity. Right afterward, however, I saw myself standing in the playground, in the middle of the gray gravel surface littered with crumpled-up sandwich wrappings, a fat, ten-year old girl with very large, round eyes, all by herself. The other children were walking around in groups or in pairs, some with their arms around each other, others playing pranks on one another, and still others throwing colored balls back and forth. Now my double began to move, too, taking a few awkward steps, probably encumbered by the heavy splint, calling out in all directions without getting an answer and stretching out her arms in vain toward the other children. The whole scene, repeated several times ad nauseum, made me sad. To see myself in such a shameful situation was embarrassing and annoying, all the more so since I don't remember such an occurrence from my school days at all.

84

Asked Attendant No. 3 about the meaning of the scene at the playground. This time he was sociable and communicative, telling me that at that time I had not hit *the right note* and for that reason had not been able to sing in the big choir. Things I didn't mean to say had always slipped out somehow: smart, insolent remarks instead of friendly words, spite instead of kindness, and so on, which can so easily lead to a kind of ostracism. He went on at length about this matter; it would appear that he has a special interest in adolescent psychology. Although I don't dislike him quite as much as I did in the beginning, I'm having a hard time understanding him. I mean, it's hard for me to see the connection between his explanations and my experiences in the House. While talking with him quite sensibly, I nevertheless always remain the child I was transformed into that morning – the child whose loneliness weighs on me like a heavy burden. In addition, I feel that I'm getting more and more tired as the days go by and that I have less and less resistance to bring to bear on my experiences in the museum. At noon today I noticed with trepidation that the waiter tore off the page from the calendar and that the new date appeared, December 23.

85

I can't go on any longer. Although I really had the best intentions of going through with my studies in the House of Childhood, I feel that I can't do it anymore. This last episode (in the playground) is not at all to blame for my breakdown, however. It's more that I'm worn out (thanks to the museum's strange methods), ground down, and no longer capable of going through with this sort of thing. In the final analysis, no one can force me to visit the research institute from now on. Except for my initial reluctance, I did go there voluntarily, so now I can also choose to stay away voluntarily. The material I've collected so far, and which I don't even dare to read one more time in my present condition, is probably of some value. I don't have to worry about not being able to publish it and for that reason not being able to pay the waiter. It's true that the story of my journey of self-discovery comes to a bad end this way, I mean, ends with a defeat, a break. But I finally owe it to myself (and not just to myself) to call a halt to these activities as long as I'm still able to. My present decisiveness I owe more than anything to Carl. When I think about the fact that I'll still see him today, I suddenly feel very happy and content. He'll give me a big hug, and I'll talk or not talk. Maybe from now on we won't even be apart again but live together as he's been wanting to do for so long. As soon as I get back from town (after all, I'll have to leave this place to make my phone call), I'll pack my bags and get my books and notes together and put them in a safe place. The waiter will simply have to light his little ethereal Christmas tree for himself. When the pink candles burn, I'll be far away. What a relief to be grown up and in charge of my own life.

86

It's late at night, and I'm still here. I haven't packed my things either, nor have I called a cab. The waiter seems not to have expected anything to the contrary although I did give him all kinds of hints when I went out to make my call. He prepared my dinner and set the table at the usual time. He was exceptionally attentive today, kept running all over the place, and when I was sitting there terribly depressed with my head in my hands waiting for dinner to be served, I listened to his comings and goings, his light, tired, but infinitely obliging steps. After dinner, he brought me today for the first time a hot-water bottle, a really old-fashioned copper container with a light-blue wool cover. I shouldn't be surprised if he had crocheted this cover himself. Although he's so good at shoveling snow, he seems totally asexual, and his clean-shaven face sometimes resembles the delicate and bloodless face of an old woman.

Carl has gone away on a trip, they told me on the phone. He left no address and won't be back till the middle of March.

87

I've given in to the waiter's suggestion and taken a few days rest. I'm dead tired, and the museum will be closed for the holidays anyway, he thinks. For my entertainment the waiter has selected a couple of books, among them some yellowed and mildewed issues of an old magazine called *Across Land and Sea,* which are stitched together in one big, fat volume. This volume is worth reading for its smell alone (like the musty drawers in an old summer house). Besides, it contains stories written in a style that you just don't see anymore. One in particular, which was called "Gina Ginori," appealed to me. The heroine of this story is a young girl who is actually dead but acts as if she were alive, and she is constantly surrounded by the smell of lilies and corpses. Because of my physical condition, I'm actually not capable of really reading or even judging what is so fascinating about this work, which may be rather inferior from a literary point of view. I'm lying on the bed in my room, leafing through this thick volume and waiting for the waiter to call me for the lighting of the little Christmas tree. I guess he'll have his Christmas after all now, as well as the surprise, which I can't really say I'm looking forward to.

88

I do hereby declare that the objects I have left behind in my room in the upper story of the coffeehouse, including the jewelry located in the drawer of the nightstand, shall belong to the waiter and that he may dispose of them as he sees fit. I owe him much gratitude for all his help, especially for his special attention on Christmas Eve, and under no circumstances would I wish to see him suffer any material loss because of my presence here in this House.

89

I wrote the foregoing declaration yesterday shortly before going to bed. The clock was just striking twelve, the hour at which midnight mass begins in the Catholic churches. The waiter had extinguished the candles, which were still burning —

since they apparently weren't made of wax but of a longer-lasting substance – and he had given me the last one, still lit, so that I could find my way to my room. I didn't wonder in the least at the fact that he didn't turn on the electric light again. As I listened to the bells, I sat down for a moment at the table and wrote, holding the candle in my left hand.

90

The surprise that the waiter had in store for me last night was an old-fashioned doll's house, which he had dragged out of God only knows what old chest. I was just thrilled with this doll's house from the moment I saw it. Whereas the ordinary rooms of this kind usually are uninteresting square rooms arranged as living room or dining room with couches, buffets, grandfather clocks, and stiff, hard chairs, this house was one circular drawing room, the kind you sometimes still find in old country houses. The floor was covered with little, narrow parquet strips, and the walls were adorned with silk and decorated with small brass sconces and pretty, painted landscapes in gilt frames. The room, which was not open on one side like other doll's houses, had only one window or rather one glass door leading into a garden, which was suggested by a snow-covered lawn, some trees also covered with snow, and a Chinese lantern hung with little bells. Tiny bells also hung from the slender Christmas tree, which occupied the middle of the round room and which could be set in motion by means of a clockwork, as I found out later, so that it chimed softly while turning very slowly. It was winter outside and Christmas inside, the tables were set with white linens and loaded down with tiny toys as well as with all kinds of other miniature objects, including some pretty, flowered plates with baked goods charmingly made to look like the real thing. The chairs and little couches as well as the dainty tables had legs that were beautifully wrought, and the cushions were embroidered with flowers and vines in a tiny cross-stitch pattern. Best of all, however, the pretty room was inhabited by lots of little figures, children and grownups, crowding around the tree, and even very old people in shabby clothes who had to lean against the walls or a piece of furniture because their legs wouldn't carry them.

The reader won't be at all surprised to hear that I immediately began playing with these little figures, leading the children to their tables and engaging the grownups in conversation with each other: for as old as I am, I've never lost my joy of playing, and in bringing up my children I was of some use, at least in the sense that I could invent numerous games and devote myself completely to them. So, the waiter had scarcely cleared the dining table and put the little pavilion in front of me before I was reaching out for the charming figures. I might just mention that I did notice the old man tiptoeing out of the room and turning out the light at the door so that the little candles from the Christmasy advertising gimmick placed on the mantle could brighten the marvelous scene so much the better. Time just flew as I busily distributed gifts for the children, the grownups, and the countless poor people who had been invited to the party. Finally, I just sat there in silence, listening to the fine chiming of the tree in the doll's house that was turning with its tiny bells and casting its little shadow over the sparkling things, the neat little dolls and the silk-shimmering walls. I don't remember anymore what I was thinking about. I only know that I had forgotten all my fears of the past days and felt completely happy.

91

The doll's house has disappeared, and the waiter has also removed the little white snowflake tree. I feel a lot better than before the holidays and have decided to continue my studies in the museum. The fact that I'm so full of courage again stems not only from the fact that Christmas Eve went off so much better than I had thought. As far as I remember, I always suffered from depression during the period before Christmas, but it stopped mysteriously as soon as the days grew longer again. My belief that the purely astronomical occurrence of the solstice affects the physical and mental well-being of people is so strong that I imagine I can already perceive a change in the light today toward the March-like, the spring-like. I would really like to go for a walk on the outskirts of town. If I work extra hard for a few days, maybe I could squeeze out time for a break like that. As I learned from the waiter, the nearest stop of the new "door-to-door" express is supposed to be located on the main street near the large department store. Plantation No. 315 (Password: Forest Joy) can be reached from there in a few minutes, and there's enough time before the return trip to take a nice walk and smell the earth, which must be workable since there's still a thaw. I'm really looking forward to this walk. There's always something artificial, stagy, about the scenery shown in the museum. The fact that one's alive can be confirmed only by the present, never by the past.

92

Today I found everything in the House changed, and in the most peculiar way. One can best compare the kind of treatment I'm receiving there now with that of a sailor boy after his baptism at the equator or quite generally with that of any adolescent who has his initiation rites behind him. One might also draw on the mysteries of antiquity for comparison, with their journeys through deep darkness intensified by all kinds of scary creatures, through the night toward the light. Still, it would be an exaggeration to claim that I find nothing but brightness and clarity in the H.O.C. It's just that a fresher wind is blowing, as in a classroom when you've got a new teacher with a more pleasant personality than the one you had before. More than anything, it's that they've changed their methods. As soon as I've entered the House now, I'm asked by the custodian to say anything that comes to mind, a word or a name, and he immediately shows me the corresponding items or persons. The reader will understand that I much prefer this current method of teaching to the earlier one. Instead of being haunted by the most unpleasant images without being able to do anything about it, I'm now able to select what I want, which gives me a strong feeling of freedom. Another innovation, namely the introduction of certain amusing features, is equally welcome. I'll try to familiarize the reader with these new instructional methods tonight by giving an example.

93

Here's an example of the novel pictorial instruction being used now at the H.O.C. On the way to the museum I think of the words *Cacol, Diavolo,* and *Carmen.* Asked by the custodian to name one of them, I choose the last one which, I believe, has some connection with my grandfather on my mother's side. Sure enough, they show me my grandfather, but in the most astonishing way. For he is sitting in the middle of a circus ring filled with dark-brown malt grain instead of with sand, and he is playing the piano. Around him there are several large contraptions, whose steel arms, clawlike hands, and brush fingers pick up, rinse, and put down again small casks, while a line of large horses dressed in leather aprons prance around the outer circle of the ring. The scene changes in a flash, now you're at the opera. My grandfather is still drumming away with his short fingers, but this time on the red velvet parapet of his loge. He's singing along: "Fight on, torero." All heads turn. I'm sitting next to him, so ashamed. New scene change. Now he's walking in the street with his hands in the pockets of his topcoat, quickly, impatiently, a short person with the face of a French petit bourgeois, sad puppy's eyes, very much alone. Attendant No. 2 commented at length on all this, concentrating on the Founding Period, which I'm going to skip here because you can read up on this period (the last decades of the past century) in any reference work. He further mentioned the name Felix Mottl (apparently a very famous conductor at the time) and added that my grandfather, aside from his appointment to the court, had also owned a brewery and had been involved in heavy speculation with various properties on the outskirts of town, but that he had lost all his money to inflation and died a poor man. What moved me strangely were the street names he had picked out for the new development (Siegfried, Ortrud, Fafnir), which he got from the Ring of the Nibelung and which supposedly still exist at the site of the former resi-dence.

94

The entertaining method of instruction continues. From a purely technical point of view, we're talking about a kind of montage, this juxtaposition of objects that really don't belong together, like the style of a certain method of painting that came into fashion even before the First World War and that has remained more or less alive up until the middle of our century. For example, at the word "Diavolo" my father appeared, a young man still, who made a light hourglasslike object roll and dance on a string stretched between two short rods. But when he suddenly pulled the string taut and made the marvelous thing fly high up into the air, it was a falcon that never returned and that my father followed with his eyes for the longest time, as the light bamboo rods in his hands were slowly covered with the leaves and flowers of an exotic vine, a blue convolvulus. Attendant No. 2 also wanted to give his explanation of this scene, which had to do with certain Romantic inclinations on the part of my father (Capodimonte, Frederic II of Hohenstaufen), but I interrupted him in the rudest way. I have the feeling that images like that are best left uninterpreted and that a stranger is hardly qualified to comment on personal matters of that nature.

95

The tasks required of me in the H.O.C. lately have also been of shorter duration so that I give in to them now without anger, even with a certain pleasure. Today my job was to redecorate a room, that is, I had to select specific items (where and when?) that would go together from a warehouse that was stuffed with pieces of furniture, rugs, drapes, etc. The memory of a family scene they had shown me when I first started my studies offered me a clue. A living room papered with dark-blue burlap was the location of this family scene, as you'll recall. A piece of furniture from the period of the first French empire, a kind of filing cabinet with classical pediment, drawers lined with vellum, and bronze fittings and rings, was absolutely essential, as were a shallow writing desk and a china cabinet that had the same severe form and showed the same ornamentation. Choosing the other objects was much more difficult and took me a disproportionately long time, especially the drapes (I finally decided on burgundy velvet with matching cotton stripes). I don't want you to get the idea that all this redecorating took place as in real life, that is, with the moaning and groaning of heavily burdened movers. Everything in the House is a mirage, a game, ease to the highest degree. Whatever item I wanted, changed its location soundlessly and as if by magic. Whatever I rejected returned to the warehouse in the same way. Eventually, the room was done to my liking. Only one corner remained kind of empty, on the desk several items were lacking, and a suitable picture could not be found for a faded spot on the wall.

96

Read the newspapers again for the first time in ages. The usual New Year's retrospectives and predictions, also some prophesying, death of a famous person, spaceship disaster, etc. In addition, the news that a festival committee for the celebration of the still rather distant year 2000 has already been formed, and an international one at that. All countries apparently are bent on promoting moral rearmament to such an extent by this time as to show off the "One World" as a fait accompli in the eyes of history in this anniversary year. Their solemn proclamation is supposed to be made on January 1, 2000. Unfortunately they cannot agree on the place for the celebration. Since both old Europe and all the other parts of the world are making claims, arrangements are being made to transfer the celebration to an extraterrestial site. In addition, concerns are already being raised to the effect that the new year wouldn't begin on the day they've decided on at all but rather on January 1, 2001. As Attendant No. 2 (who seems to be bored in the H.O.C. and for that reason has taken to stopping by to chat in the coffeehouse) just told me, the same heated debate took place at the beginning of the last century. Still, today there seems to be an ulterior motive at the bottom of this last-mentioned theory, namely the pessimistic tendency to believe that this cannot be accomplished, that is, the wish to gain some time to achieve this noble goal.

97

Something amusing in the H.O.C. again: a line of life-size female puppets coming in through the one door of the projection room as if on tracks, then slowly hobbling past by fits and starts only to disappear again through another door. They are made of wax or of papier mâché but are amazingly lifelike and carry little signs with their names: Mademoiselle Berthe, Mademoiselle Flore, Miss Barker, Miss Cacol, and Fräulein Wucherpfennig. The custodian informs me that all of these ladies were our governesses. He claims that the surly Mademoiselle Berthe always eavesdropped at the door; that the pretty, consumptive Mademoiselle Flore gave my parents insolent answers; that Miss Barker read aloud to my older sisters at night a most unsuitable novel, *The Mess of Pottage,* which she herself had written; and that the funny Miss Cacol had lain down on a park lawn with me and then to my delight given the policeman a totally false address. These stories cheered me up although I couldn't stop wondering about my parents' choices. Fräulein Wucherpfennig, about whom the custodian only reported that before she arrived my mother had called us together and sworn us to chivalry, was the last to appear and stopped for just a moment with rattling clockwork motor, and I watched with strange emotion her tiny form, marred by an enormous hump, and her delicate, pointed face radiating as if with noble fervor.

98

The purely theoretical instruction currently on the program in the H.O.C. is given by Attendant No. 3. Today he drew three boxes on the board for me. The first was empty, the second one shaded very dark, the third one lightly shaded halfway across while the other half was merely outlined. The attendant put Roman numerals above the little boxes, writing the words "Security" and "Altercation" under the first two and "Growing Insight" under the shaded half of the third. I'm assuming that this graphic presentation indicates that the material will be studied in different phases. To this first phase (Roman Numeral One, Security) apparently belong the images they've shown me of the music box, the kaleidoscope, the garden, etc., whereas the ugly fear and loneliness experiences that I was forced to repeat form the contents of the second box. The fact that I'm staying in the first half of the third phase for the time being, in accordance with the now apparently strictly kept chronological sequence, also occurs to me. But I feel an intense dislike for the all too strict divisions of the different phases, and besides I'm dying to know what's waiting for me in the third box and whether or not the attendant in the end will not shade this temporarily unmarked field black, too. I couldn't drag any explanation out of him on this subject; as a matter of fact, he was strangely laconic during this whole lesson.

99

Felt a real need to talk to Carl about the theoretical instruction and genuinely wanted to have him around; also worried about him. Strange, though, how I have been feeling lately that time is standing still, whereas entire decades are passed through in the H.O.C., as if I, very tired after a long trip, would find everything there totally unchanged. How often have I gone out without paying much attention to the time and come home late with a bad conscience, all hot from running, only to find Carl, absorbed in his work, just looking up and asking in a friendly voice: "What – back so soon?"

100

The museum management has given the lie to itself, that is, to its theory of growing clarity and perspicuity. A horrible scene was prepared for me today, namely the suicide of a young man with the face of a child (presumably my cousin) who was lying on the carpet of the so-called master's study with his brains spilling out as a result of a gunshot wound, his fingers clutching a farewell letter. All the while I see this young man in the same state sitting upright at a table, ghostlike, while devilishly grinning characters deal cards, and his polite child's face smiles as they collect the money lying in a heap of gold pieces in front of him. Apparently an incident had been reenacted here that I hadn't witnessed myself but that I had imagined back then from stories I had overheard. Another image intervened: my cousin's mother, petite, blonde, and fair, riding on the train through olive groves, a newspaper on her lap and in front of her on his knees a young, dark-haired conductor clutching her hands, her fists hammering away at the newspaper while she screams incomprehensibly at him and weeps, mumbling the same words over and over again: That's my son. The scene touched me deeply. There was no trace of the calm perspicuity, of the joviality, of the tasks that were pleasant to solve anymore, only disgust with the mortal wound, only fear of darkness, of evil, of whatever had destroyed that honorable but foolish young man. No commentary, only an indistinct droning voice that warned against playing cards, against debts, and against bad company – all of it as from a long-forgotten era that one probably knows only from books.

101

Music without pictures as if over a loudspeaker, recitation of poetry in between. I noticed very soon that here a definite musical-literary experience was not repeated, that they were more intent on making me listen to my former favorite pieces of music and poetry in a kind of potpourri, perhaps in an attempt to blot out the latest unpleasant impression. Actually, it was a fairly random combination of instrumental music, singing, and recitation, varied enough. I still liked much of it, some of it less, but during the entire concert each selection made me feel curiously homesick, the way you feel about your own only partly understood stirrings of love. Neither the coolness of the distance in time nor a certain literary arrogance determined by the current art trend is any match for it: For I have borne it for seven years, and now I can bear it no more, the old rebellious vassal, Archibald Douglas, who reins in his monarch's charger, the magic name of the castle Linlithgow, which simply doesn't rhyme with any German word. But you can't criticize, you don't want to. *Death and the Maiden,* Schubert's quartet with the death agony motif, not bad taste, you know, but right after this is *Roses from the South* hammered out on a player piano. And was this any less moving, less touchingly beautiful? "They do not eat, they do not drink, and on their ship the lights don't blink" a chorus sang, and the custodian whispered what I already knew to start with: *The Flying Dutchman* Finally, my mother's voice singing *the song.* She accompanied herself on the piano, which I recognized from a certain carefree way of attacking the keys that she had, but also from an extraordinary musical stressing of the lower notes, even on the piano. And then the children's voices chimed in, three not altogether pure but wildly enthusiastic ones, and one tender one, clear as a bell. The song of our childhood, Napoleon's two grenadiers talking about their emperor on their way back from Russia. The Marseillaise . . .

102

Sometimes I'm happy after all that there are attendants in the H.O.C. Although they usually don't have anything to say that amounts to anything, and although their didactic way of speaking gets on my nerves, as does their habit of never answering a question directly, there are times when it's possible to learn something from them. Attendant No. 2 held forth today on the alienation that so many people feel, because I had asked him about the Marseillaise (in the home of a Prussian officer!), and it soon became clear that he had my father in mind. He related this being on the outside to a desire to stray from your own, frequently too confining circumstances and the impossibility of feeling completely at home in the new environment. In addition, he said, the outsider suffers from a continuous, powerful tension between the desire for freedom and the will to subordination, a subordination that is considered ethical behavior in its own right again and again without any real testing of the object. Inherited abilities, also inherited political tendencies, as well as a personal artistic bent that is not nurtured to achieve any real creativity, simply sharpen the conflict, which, however, under certain circumstances remains hidden behind the overall impression of a congenial, even fascinating personality. The attendant wanted to go into detail about the history of the region where I come from (the Baden Revolution of 1848, Herwegh, etc.), which held a special interest for him as a historian, and he started to establish some connection between it and my father's character. But he thought better of it when he noticed how unpleasant it was for me to see my father's personality taken apart in this cold and objective manner. "Want to know which bust was the only one in your parents' home?" he asked. And when I answered yes to his question, he led me into a kind of storeroom with tall, rough-hewn bookshelves. On the shelves were several sculptures of marble, bronze, cast iron, and plaster, as presumably were to be found in middle-class homes during the first decades of our century: Bismarck and

Wilhelm II, The Thorn Puller, and Princess Nefertiti, also a female death mask which bore the puzzling inscription "Incon-
nue de la Seine." The bust that the attendant wanted to show
me had been put up on a portable stand as if it had already been
determined that it would be displayed soon. I had no sooner
caught sight of it when I ran up to it, stroked its smooth, finely
veined marble cheeks and, as if he were a favorite uncle of
mine, greeted this stern old fellow, who with a mocking smile
stuck out his wrinkled old-man's neck from his phony, classical
drapery. Then I spelled out, in the usual childish way I had in
the H.O.C., the name etched into the pedestal: VOLTAIRE.

103

My physical condition has improved so much in the last few
days that I'm thinking of taking up my journalistic pursuits
again. There are certain things in public life that you can't leave
unexplored, like the ridiculous speculations about cosmic
property, for example, which I read about in the paper today.
Although the occupancy of the moon that was announced a
long time ago hasn't taken place yet, many firms have already
been formed for the purpose of exploiting the deposits of pri-
mary matter presumed to exist there, and they have raised sub-
stantial amounts of money among their shareholders. The lists
of emigrants that each country projects for itself without any
regard for certain necessary quotas are already oversubscribed
here – lately they've been considering the establishment of a
special office for construction on the moon. In this regard, the
legal implications for all these organizations remain totally un-
clear. Besides, it's frightening how many people are ready to
leave our planet for good, especially since the enormous cost of
going makes it unthinkable for most people to return. Even the
most desolate areas of Australia or South America have some-

thing in common with the birthplaces of Dante, Cervantes, or Goethe, namely the universe. Even the antipodes of Homer's heroes were subject to the magnetism of the same planet. Only the cosmic desire to emigrate gives us the absolute, painful proof of how slight the need is for the old, cultural heritage or for any cultural feelings whatsoever, and how we may count on a total rootlessness in the future, maybe in a positive sense as well.

104

I'm glad to report that the feeling of happiness I experienced during my first days in the H.O.C. (Attendant No. 3 would call it Phase Roman Numeral One) does occasionally still return. Today I experienced a whole bunch of impressions, a rushing back and forth in distant rooms, during which I never lost the spell of bliss for one moment. The password this time was "eyeball," a term that at first didn't seem to have any connection with the things that appeared. The charmed circle included the narrow meadow valley with its forests, in which the approach of a wanderer (that is, a pedestrian) was heralded by the barking of assorted farm dogs, at first far away, then closer and closer. The bowling ball, which is hanging on a rope and on which I sit swinging through the air, from the wall of the stables to the shrubbery of fir trees, from the terrace chatter of the grownups to the solemn twilight of the hayloft; the stone quarry, a high pile of irregularly hewn blocks of granite that I'm climbing on: not enough grip, growing anxiety, finally, right below the dark-blue sky the roots that I can grab hold of, and on the plateau the rough pillows of heather that I plunge into, the tufts of grass, wet with dew, cool on my face; the ruby-red glass jar (the "eyeball") filled with honey that you could get out with a spoon, not golden and runny but greenish gray, raw and tough but with golden dots in it like little bees in the sunlight, treasure houses imbued with the fragrance of the deep forest, pine needles, resin, and hay; the well of all wells, a little trough of granite slabs covered with moss that the water empties into from the depths of the mountain across a piece of bark, clear as the moon, inexhaustible, and you can hold your hands under it, a small, veined vessel, and drink from it and let go of it again, and right away the music from the valley, which has been silent for a moment, soars again, these soft, pure tones that are not shattered by any motor noise . . .

105

The fact that the spirit of the Enlightenment (both of the eighteenth and the nineteenth century) ruled in my family has already been made clear to me, and certainly not just by making the bust of Voltaire available. But an event called forth by me today, actually through the words *Immanuel* and *Prince of Peace*, which I had just thought of, nevertheless illustrated, at least for me, a way of hearing and seeing that deviated strongly from that kind of rationalism. I was attending a church service, in an Evangelical church, as a matter of fact, which my grandfather had switched to when he was quite old, as the custodian informed me. The service was rendered true to form in every detail: the pastor in the pulpit with his clerical neckband, great big hymnals with gilt edges on the lecterns, the congregation, dressed in black or at least dark clothing, in the pews with their funereal faces. The fact that I didn't understand a word of the pastor's sermon, although I was sitting quite close to the pulpit, the fact that his words more or less passed over me, as in a room with poor acoustics, but at the same time were quite audible and yet completely impossible to understand whereas individual words and sentences from the liturgy sounded perfectly clear, as if spoken by an entirely different voice, all this can only mean that at the time I heard nothing other than just these words, which incidentally fill me with fear and delight even today. They didn't actually seem to have anything to do with the church but welled from a much deeper source and with primitive force while returning to it without being any the worse for wear. From those words and phrases I've retained the following: Our Father. Sitting at the right hand of the Lord from whence he shall come to judge the living and the dead. May he shine his countenance upon you and give you peace. The power and the glory forever. At the end of the service a hymn was sung which also moved me, although it completely lacked any such archaic loftiness. It began with the question "Where doth the soul find its home, its peace," and preceding the self-provided response "Up there in the light" at great, plaintive intervals was a painfully deliberate "no, no; no, no; not here."

106

When taking an oath in a court of law, you're asked to tell the truth, the whole truth, and nothing but the truth, if I remember right. This most justifiable request is not fulfilled in the "House of Childhood" museum. At my last experience in the H.O.C. (the Evangelical service), I was about eleven years old, as far as I can tell from my height, my dress, and my spiritual development. Since one's actual childhood may be considered at an end by the age of twelve or thirteen, I must assume that the number of things I'm yet to be shown is limited and that my studies will be over in the foreseeable future. This thought, which came to me as soon as I woke up this morning, frightened me. Was it possible that the whole truth of my life as a child had been expressed in these few images and emotions? Didn't the museum find anything else in my past, or didn't it consider anything else worth keeping or representing, as it were? It would be easy to figure out the number of days I lived through; it must be several thousand. Were most of them, in fact, nothing but pages in a calendar that a hand tears off and throws in the wastebasket, one by one or in bunches, as the case may be? I admit that the reexperiencing of many thousand days as a child would be boring, even unbearable, but I feel about the experiences put before me the way I feel about letters or pages in a journal which, after having been shortened as the publisher sees fit, begin and end with little dots – leaving me with the thought that the most essential things are hiding behind those ellipses. Incidentally, in the museum there is as little regard for speaking "nothing but the truth" as for speaking "the whole truth." Surely, I've never seen my father as I did at noon today in the hospital with terribly frightening eyes peering out from under a white bandage on his head. A much later report of my mother's, in which, by the way, there was no talk at all about a head injury but rather about a deep depression on the part of my father, must have given the museum management the wrong idea.

107

I did not order the film that the custodian had someone show me today. It bore the year 1914, and the showing of it was forced upon me, even to the point of having the doors locked to the outside for the first time. Of course, I could have closed my eyes, and I did that for a while, simply as a sign of protest if nothing else, but certainly not the whole time. I'm curious by nature, and it interested me for scientific reasons if for none other to learn why the museum considered it so important for me to view this particular film. In any case, it wasn't until the very end that this became evident. These quickly changing images were exclusively mass scenes that had been taken at railway stations and in streets and squares in a big city. For the

most part, you saw soldiers in old-fashioned uniforms marching through the city with girls, women, and children on their
arms, and garlands of flowers on their helmets, guns, and bayo-
nets. Others, just as dressed up, leaned out of the windows of
long trains, while a crowd of enthusiastic civilians screamed
and shouted with joy. The whole time there was singing and
playing of brass instruments and beating on drums. It was like
a huge celebration of joy with people throwing themselves in
each other's arms, singing, laughing, and waving flags, only
that at the end a song was heard, sung by men's voices and accompanied by the muffled steps of marching feet across the
steppes, completely void of people, above which an occasional
black cross could be seen – a song like of birds in a forest, of
one's home and the hope of seeing one's loved ones again, a
song that made you feel a lump in your throat that was simply
impossible to suppress.

108

I don't know whether or not the last phase has begun, I know
only that since I was forced to watch the war film there's no
longer any question of free will in the H.O.C. I'm no longer
consulted, only dragged along and whirled around – as if they
were suddenly anxious to get rid of me. The images come
quickly now, one after the other: street, school, home, everything transformed, city without end, tall buildings, throngs of
people rushing by on their way somewhere. My road to school,
fascinating between casket shops and secondhand stores, the
overhead railway hissing as it disappears into the earth, forbid-
den trips to the large department store on the corner, the smell
of food and perfume, the smiling masks of the life-size mannequins, the feeling of adventure and the world's abundance. In
school, other faces, the twitching one of the headmistress, the

white-bearded one of the math teacher, the blackboard with its mysteriously severe forms: circles, triangles, ellipses, drawn with colored chalk. Theater, dark abyss full of whispering, the beating of a gong, curtain, deep below the room in the tower with its telescope and indistinct figures, small, far away, yet near, a voice that takes your breath away: "Enough of that, Seni, come on down now." All the while a choir is singing, but it's a choir of hoodlums, smart-alecky, indifferent: "a corpse was floating in the Landwehr canal." And then it's winter, knitting room, winding field-gray, scratchy wool, early morning, lacing up of boots in the cold, dark room, textbook and bread with beet marmalade next to the displayed foot. Hurdy-gurdy across the black crust of snow, piano practice, Clementi sonata, and, stuck between two bars of the iron fence in our front yard, the head of my little brother, his face covered with tears, getting thicker and redder, a fear like all the others, but this time everything is different. This time you can say: soon, soon someone will be here to saw through the bars, soon, soon everything will be all right again . . .

109

The calendar that used to hang by the mirror in the coffeehouse has disappeared and hasn't been replaced with a new one for this year. Since the newspapers are no longer delivered on a regular basis but simply brought by the waiter in big bundles as waste sheets, I have no idea what today's date is; in fact, I can't even say for sure what month it is. Since the big snowstorm, which was most unusual and can only be considered a technical failure in this day and age of weather simulations, we haven't had any wintry weather. Maybe it's precisely the mild temperatures that are to blame for the fact that the waiter is ill, suffers from rheumatism or arthritis, and barely drags himself around with a pale face. He refuses help, though, and even insists on continuing to wait on me. Instead of complaining about his own condition, he worries about my health, frets about my poor appearance, and takes pains to prepare foods, lately even meat, that give me strength. Actually, I haven't been feeling too good for the last couple of days. All that commotion in the House is getting to me. Sometimes I think I'm in a kind of roller coaster car where you never know what's hidden behind the closed doors that you're racing toward. I've been hearing shooting lately – a sense-impression that can only be based on deception since the First Great War wasn't really waged in this country, nor, for the most part, was there any bombardment of the cities. On the whole, I have the impression that they're trying to confuse me on purpose, the way you give someone with his eyes covered up a couple of turns before starting to play blindman's buff.

110

Today no show and tell, also no theory, but instead a remedial course like the ones I had earlier. Just like that other time at the very beginning of my studies, I was sitting in a boat, gliding across the black lake, across a calm sea, only this time I wasn't dreaming, and the other passengers were clearly visible: my brother and two girls my own age, one with coal-black hair and a tendency to buck teeth and the other with brown hair around her rosy face. On a big piece of brown wrapping paper, which I was holding on my knees, a map had been drawn in my hand: blue water, brown mountains, green stripes for the shores, canals and bridges, a topographical survey with fantastic names of the region we were going through, discoverers and conquerors of an enchanted land, which the many-armed water surface (according to the custodian, a small lake in the Berlin Zoo) had been transformed into for us. A rented boat, paid for in advance, one hour's worth of rowing – how ridiculous those explanations seemed today. The canal with its willows overhead *was* the Eridanos River. When we landed on the modest little island, we set foot on an undiscovered continent, and the tame swan, fed a hundred times over with leftover school sandwiches, was, as it suddenly rose up with spread-out wings, the Lord of the Crystal Mountain, the enemy . . .

III

Just as on the first night I spent in the little room upstairs in the coffeehouse, I had the feeling last night that I was in the H.O.C. I suddenly woke up for no apparent reason and noticed that the room was changed, larger, with three white iron beds, in one of which I myself was lying. I knew right away that I had better not move, in fact, that I had better act as if I were asleep or weren't there at all. You see, my sisters, whose beds were next to mine, were still awake and, instead of turning on the electric light, they had lighted two small candles that they had snitched from my birthday cake, as I noticed right away. By the light of these small, red candles, my sisters were taking turns reading aloud while lying next to each other on their stomachs with their heads close together. Their faces had an expression that they never had in the daytime, and their voices sounded totally different from their normal voices. Although they quite obviously were reading aloud from a book lying open before them, they acted as if they themselves had just now invented what they read, as if it came out of their own heads. My eldest sister said, "which has an angel at its gate, I bear its mighty, broken wing so heavy on my shoulder blade, and on my forehead as a seal its star." And my second-eldest sister said, "and always wander in the night, for I brought love into the world," and my eldest sister said, "oh, Lord, wrap your cloak around me, for in your goblet I am but the dregs, and when the last surviving soul spills the earth," and so on, all incomprehensible and thrilling, an extraordinary voice that had found its way into our home without having anything to do with my parents. A fascinating voice that they wanted to exclude me from and that I nevertheless eavesdropped on with my heart in my throat, between sleep and sleep.

112

The terrible experiences in Phase Roman Numeral Two seem to recur or to recommence on a different level. Today I took the usual route to the conservatory with my brother: gray woolen coats, music-cases, through the little park with the white statue, across the bridge, hot gray streets, market stalls, academy, stairs and corridors full of subdued, chaotically pealing music. In a room facing the courtyard, music dictation, chords being struck on the piano in tricky intervals that you have to put down on staff paper like birds on telegraph wires. In front of the window, soft chestnut foliage, fire wall, no glimpse of sky, then suddenly a thing, a large, weird thing, plunging past the window from above, which you hear hitting the pavement down in the courtyard a few seconds later. The teacher tears his hands away from the keyboard and shouts that someone has fallen off the roof, and all the children throw down their pencils but are kept away from the window and pushed out into the corridor instead where the big, musty-smelling felt doors are suddenly all standing open. It was the secretary from the office, the older students say, pressing their violins under their arms and gesticulating wildly with their bows. The humpbacked secretary who was in love with the director and who was let go today . . . and, of course, she didn't fall off the roof, no, she jumped out the window from the homeroom of class VII B, which happened to be empty at the time. They make us stand in the dark corridor for the longest time (probably until the police have evaluated the case and taken the body away), and the whole time I hear the humpbacked secretary running up the stairs in her high-heeled shoes through the empty classroom and tearing open the window, her body hitting the ground down below, only to get up again and start the whole thing over.

113

Today they showed me a funeral among other things in the film from 1912, which they had picked out without a great deal of thought. The affair was highly theatrical, it even had a certain sinister majesty. The four horses that were pulling the glass hearse with its black and silver canopy resembled medieval jousting horses, all draped in black and with big ostrich plumes on their heads. The huge coffin, also black and silver, was covered almost completely with wreaths trailing grotesque bows with gold lettering. The team of horses as well as the funeral procession that followed it moved at an incredible snail's pace. Out of brass instruments came woeful, painfully slow music. The whole thing seemed very strange: although the funeral subway system (the "Corpse Express" in the vernacular) has been in existence for only a few years, people have gotten used to seeing these inconspicuous-looking railroad cars rushing by at some reckless speed on the tracks of the Metropolitana, only to disappear immediately into the tunnels to the cemeteries.

114

Did gymnastics this afternoon, that is, practiced back flips on the rings, did pull-ups, etc., alone in a long, narrow corridor. The door to the kitchen was open, as was the door to the nurs-

ery, where my sisters were sitting at the table doing their homework. In the front room my mother was singing Schubert's *The
Brook* (it's interesting to note that I don't have to have titles like
that explained anymore; on the contrary, they have now become one with the things experienced.) I had, as I already mentioned, certain routines to execute, especially one where, after
getting up speed, I had to let the upper part of my body fall
backward and swing my legs over my head so that I could fly
through the corridor like a so-called candle, which caused my
long hair to brush the floor with a strange noise. I had to stay in
this uncomfortable, indeed unnatural position for a long time,
which was not at all unpleasant. In fact, I had a feeling of vol-
untary isolation and solitude, flew into it like a demon that will
have no part of human activities. The fact that all items in the
lighted rooms stood on their head made them strange and powerless at the same time, and that it was up to me to transform
them in this way gave me a feeling of freedom and happiness.

115

They have just confirmed once again the suspicion I've been
harboring for quite some time, that the so-called golden age of
my childhood was a myth. This time they had constructed (or
reflected through mirrors? The techniques used in the museum
are still a puzzle) a section of town that I was not familiar with.
I was roaming around that area, although I had surely been in-
structed not to go there. In front of me, in the busy crowd of
people, walked a bloated, fat woman, still young, with a puffy,
pale, almost bluish shimmering face. She was walking very
slowly and carefully with her arms stretched out to the sides, as
if her bone structure were not firm, and as if her large feet were
filled with air. Once in a while I would see her face in one of the
display windows. It was flat like a pancake, with wide, blood-

less lips and colorless eyes, which she seemed to keep open only with great difficulty. Since she was moving so slowly, I could easily have passed her and left her behind, but I didn't want to. I wasn't going anywhere special and had nothing better to do than to walk behind her and not let her out of my sight. But it didn't last long, ten steps, maybe a hundred steps, and around us still were the throngs of people crowding into the empty shops. And then the woman suddenly fainted, that is, she collapsed, quite gently, stretching out her arms even more to both sides, her head dangling on her chest. Hunger, said the men who were trying to support her and couldn't get her on her feet. And then suddenly all the people in the street kept uttering this one word, indifferently, whispering it, screaming it, this word that kept ringing in my ears now that I was standing by myself in the dark—a confusing, ghostlike chorus, which I never heard in real life, of course, but an acoustic montage that is right in line with the museum's tendency to exaggerate.

116

Blindman's buff. Labyrinth. Again and again I hear my mother singing in the H.O.C. now, not songs, you understand, but so-called solfeggios, that is, vocal exercises to which certain inane sentences are sung like "Have you not seen your father" or "Fritz, you're sitting on the hat." Sometimes, I also even see my mother, standing at the piano with her voice teacher, and the teacher is placing my mother's hand on her stomach or diaphragm to see if, in fact, she's breathing deeply enough. Then I'm standing outside the door again, hearing only the tones and now and then laughter and this idiotic "Have you not seen your fa-a-ather," and my father is in Russia (over there at the edge of the field two jackdaws are perching), and my mother is taking voice lessons for her amusement. She spends hours on end every day practicing, and she is always in the best mood. Who can understand it? I can't understand my mother, her zest for life, her terrible cheerfulness, her uncanny energy. When she starts singing, I hold my ears. When I hear her running through the house calling "Children, what a nice day," something goes through me like a cramp and a shudder and a feeling of hatred. And Attendant No. 3 arrives and says my mother had a tremendous will to joy even from childhood, and every night when she went to bed she would pronounce the word "morning" with beaming eyes, as if that next day were a shimmering object of value all in its own right. And Attendant No. 3 says my mother had tried all her life to hold on to happiness and had succeeded at it to an amazing degree so that everything loathsome that she had made light of really had become light, like the shadows of a thin layer of clouds that must give way to an overpowering sun. And finally, Attendant No. 3 says, she loved the sun more than anything.

117

Dark, dark. My father is there. I can't see him, but I hear his steps in the next room in the H.O.C. where he's pacing aimlessly back and forth, and his steps are sinister and foreign. I'm sitting there doing my homework, *Maid of Orleans,* and hidden under my notebook is a piece of paper that I want to write words on, my words, and then what really appears is something entirely different from what I had in mind. It simply doesn't sound right, and it isn't saying anything. And I begin to doodle, dog's ears around the letters, curlicues, fat stomachs, little men with tails. And then nothing but black, thick strips, close to one another, cover up, obliterate, only blackness, until I crush the paper into a ball and hurl it into the wastebasket. I'm sitting at the piano practicing scales in a melodic style, in countermovement, where it's difficult to coordinate your hands, and suddenly I drop my left hand and try to pick out a melody I know with my right, a tune I had forgotten, a wonderful tune. And I can't get it right and begin pounding on the keyboard with both hands, angry, dissonant chords, till someone appears at the door yelling "Are you out of your mind!" and my fingers separate again and meet, six sharps, in F sharp major.

118

Another theory session. Attendant No. 3 is drawing with chalk on the board again, this time on one that's already covered with fine lines like a fever curve. What he draws is also a curve, it begins in the middle of the linear system, goes down a little, then heads steeply upward, falls again but this time way below the line of the starting point, rises again, falls again, and begins to go up once more. It is obvious that we're not talking about a temperature chart here, and yet it is about high and low pressure, the ups and downs of a human being, and it is clear that this graphic presentation on the whole fits right in with the earlier division into small boxes. Only this picture is prettier than the former one. It looked like a double high-cresting wave, and at the same time it was in motion, making a thrust forward that actually had something promising about it. At the request of the attendant, I had to copy the line several times, didn't get any explanations but had to give information myself about its significance – a demand which immediately put me in a dull and dreary examination mood and into a state of total stupidity. The thought that the final examination might be around the corner has me worried. Besides, it's quite possible that such a test might be conducted in public and that it'll appear at the same time on television to millions of viewers, something on the order of the game show "All or Nothing," which was so

popular a few years ago. To answer just a few questions correctly wouldn't do me any good at all. The audience would
prod me like a sluggish bull in the arena to submit to that final,
all-important question, too; that is, the one at which everything won is wagered and in certain cases lost again.

119

To my surprise a lot is going on in our little street today. Music
over the loudspeaker, even garlands of artificial flowers of the
very old-fashioned kind. I found out the reason for these festiv-
ities from a speech delivered by the mayor, which was also
transmitted over the loudspeaker so that I could listen to it on
my way to the museum. As the mayor announced, tomorrow
will see the removal of the city's last existing sidewalks or foot-
paths in our cul-de-sac. This measure makes sense to everyone
– these slightly raised strips of pavement reserved for pedes-
trians have become completely deserted and obsolete in the last
decade whereas the space allotted for cars hasn't been sufficient
for quite some time. So everyone seems to be happy, although,
as so often is the case on these occasions (the last run of the out-
moded streetcar, etc.), a certain measure of sentiment still exists on the part of the public. The charm of the nevermore has
caused a number of curiosity seekers to get out of their cars
and walk up and down in a nostalgic-jovial mood, albeit
somewhat stiff-legged, on the so-called sidewalks doomed to
disappear. The movie cameras hummed, and I thought of the
fact that some of these pictures surely were destined to play a
role in the museum archives some day. I also thought of the
last horse-drawn streetcars they had shown me there, and it
seemed totally incomprehensible to me how much change a
human being can be a witness to, even without getting particularly old.

120

They didn't send me away. They didn't turn out the lights, nor did they force me to take any exam. Instead, they showed me something entirely new: a landscape as from a bird's-eye view, placed between two mountain ranges, hills sloping toward the river, with vineyards and chestnut trees, a cathedral built of red sandstone, and meadows over which lay a summer haze flooded with golden light. I recognized it all, and then again, I didn't. It was so new and fresh, raised from oblivion, like the goddess born out of foam from the sea. I saw it with the eyes of a homesick child from the big city to whom someone says: This is your home. And because I had been given the eyes of a child once more, and perhaps for the last time, the mountains were higher, the valleys deeper, the shadows of the lindens glistened more mysteriously, the bleeding Christ hung more lonesome above the fields of grain. I went for quite a few walks today, through the old home that was so familiar to me from later times, only different, along the stream and through the woods, and although everything was so powerful, I didn't feel it necessary to assert myself. Instead I could humble myself, submit to the tall, rustling trees, to the old pictures on the walls of the house, to the wooden figure of Christ in the fields of grain. And when for the first time I humbly accepted things for what they were, I, too, was accepted, a child of the old crumbling house at the edge of the mountain, a child of the old, questionable world.

121

A short time ago, I could hardly wait to get back to the museum after lunch. The same surroundings, the same feeling of happiness, only less poetic, also less general, since they had me straighten up the rooms in the house and pull weeds in the garden, stubborn weeds that had become rooted in fertile or in rocky soil, and the sun was burning and my back hurt. I was always alone, except for a couple of old workmen and the old housekeeper, the same one that bears such a strange resemblance to the waiter in the coffeehouse. I would have liked to ask Attendant No. 2 if the war was actually over now, and I would have liked to ask the custodian how it came to be that it was my job to fix up the family home, which had been uninhabitable because of its run-down condition, I, the youngest of three sisters and no older than fourteen. But nobody was around, and when I pressed the bell-pushes as I was leaving, nothing stirred.

122

Just like yesterday, only even more prosaic, since this time I was busy taking up pieces of sod in the meadow and ploughing with all ten fingers in the black soil, which was riddled with fine roots. The whole thing was a hunt, and the game was earthworms, reddish gray ones, that I picked up with loathing and placed in a small tin box with a half-ripped-off label (Muratti), whole ones or pieces, since the slippery bodies kept coming apart in my hands all the time, only to move on in segments, still wriggling. And yet I have a feeling of great impatience and expectation the whole time. I keep listening and looking around me, for whom, I wonder, for steps behind the hedgerow, for laughter, for a voice that could be either a man's or a boy's and that calls my name. For the one who will spear my earthworms on his hook and cast his line, and every once in a while it will get caught in the shrubbery on the bank of the stream, and I'll untangle it again and stand by as he quickly turns the little crank. The water will be still and dark green in the shade and will rush and glisten in the sun, and I will be on the lookout for trout, the young, reckless ones and the old ones that stay put at the bottom of the deep and notice everything. But the whole time, I would see only him, I knew that very well, and I also knew how everything would happen, only that it didn't happen yet, that it wasn't part of today's lesson, which apparently was not to include anything other than the search for earthworms and the feeling of expectation, and only at the very end and very far off, the call.

123

How happy I am this evening. Although it's late, I simply must write in my notebook, must say one more time, how much that last little episode has strengthened and encouraged me. For what was this, anyway, other than the stirrings of young love, and yet it has awakened in me the memory of all moments of bliss and security, which, come to think of it, there actually weren't so few of in the H.O.C. after all. For the first time, I also recognized the alternation between indifference and love, fear and confidence, self-assertion and devotion, which I experienced there, as a symbol of all life. Tomorrow (surely I'll experience the continuation of the brook scene) I'll see all that even more clearly. If they're planning to test me after all, then I'll be able to come up with the answers, even though it won't be in the learned manner of Attendant No. 3. I'll retract my criticism of the instructional materials and even take the position that the experiences they made me suffer through were worthwhile precisely because of their insignificance. For the life of a child is filled with the same tensions, fears, and joys that make up the life of an adult, and the small curve eventually inclines toward love.

124

Just a few words before I'm off, after breakfast – which really wasn't any breakfast at all but just a cup of old, warmed-over coffee. I won't say anything to the waiter about it, because to my surprise another guest has arrived. I hear the waiter talking to him in an excited voice, but I can't see him because he's sitting in a niche. The presence of a stranger in the coffeehouse is quite unusual. If he stays, we'll have to greet each other, maybe even talk to one another in the evenings. Most likely, he's the one who has brought the newspapers along that are lying on my table, still damp from the print, hot off the press, so to speak. Today is the twenty-first of March, the first day of spring. Since I can hardly wait to get to the museum, I haven't read the paper. I only noted with interest that they're selling spring suits already. The sun is shining outside, and the coffeehouse seems especially old-fashioned and run-down with its yellowed curtains and dusty plush furniture.

125

The museum seems to be closed although today is Wednesday, as I learned from the paper, and not any kind of state or church holiday. There was no sign to that effect, but no one opened up. I was extremely impatient and kept ringing the bell, also tried to make myself heard by knocking on the door and calling. But there was only a great, almost solemn silence, and in the bright sunshine the gray building with its walled-up windows stood as if bewitched. Actually, I spent the whole morning walking up and down in the cul-de-sac, ringing the bell and calling repeatedly. I also checked the gate that had been ajar at the very beginning, but now it was firmly locked, and nothing could be seen of the firing slit-like opening that I also had discovered then. Since museums sometimes have a way of closing down without prior warning because of restoration, I didn't give up hope. I simply had to be let in one more time. I had to see the trout stream once again as well as the boy that it was so thrilling to be waiting for. Toward noon, I went to the coffeehouse where I'm sitting now, although they're not bringing me anything to eat. I'm very hurt that the waiter not only keeps bringing the new guest (a sort of scruffy-looking older man) the most wonderful-smelling dishes but also that he had the nerve to move the little vase with primroses that was standing on my table over to his. If I didn't have just one thing in mind, namely to return to the museum, I would make it a point to find out why he's ignoring me this way, or why the new guest is so very important to him.

126

It's evening, and nothing was of any use. No entry, no possibility of talking to one of the attendants. Long, unhappy waiting around in the deserted street till the hour of twilight when a light spring haze arose between the houses and eventually covered up the sign with the inscription "House of Childhood" and the Jugendstil embellishment. Finally, back here and to my table. My books had been removed and stacked on a chair. In their place was an envelope with some writing on it, in which I thought I would find the bill, but it was a letter, and in Carl's hand. I was overjoyed to open it but didn't really read it the way I wanted to, nor did I give much thought to just how Carl had found out where I was staying. I had no sooner read the first loving words than I had this strange image, like a large ball turning slowly upward from below. And whatever was above it disappears, is torn down, a large gray building; now there's only a row of windows left, then only the ridge of the roof, then nothing. At this point, I call the waiter, who is strangely changed, suddenly has an altogether different face and walks by, two feet away from me, without hearing or seeing me, as waiters are wont to do. Since he's just about to take the new guest's suitcase to the upper story and I can't seem to get his attention, I'll copy down on a piece of paper the little paragraph from my journal concerning my legacy, which I wrote in the guest room, and put it on my table weighted down with an ashtray. When that's done, I'll leave the coffeehouse without going to the room upstairs again. I'll walk down the cul-de-sac to the main street and get on a bus there. On that short ride, I'll read my letter in peace and quiet so there'll be no time to look back in the direction of the museum, which is dark at night anyway and surely no longer recognizable.

Afterword

Marie Luise Kaschnitz was born on January 31, 1901, the daughter of a Prussian officer in an aristocratic family in Karlsruhe in southwestern Germany. She grew up in Potsdam and Berlin. In Weimar and Munich she learned the booktrade and continued working in this profession in Rome. In 1925 she married the archaeologist Guido von Kaschnitz-Weinberg, who was the director of the German Archaeological Institute in Rome. Their only child is a daughter who today lives in Berlin. With her husband, Kaschnitz spent several years in Italy, Greece, North Africa, and Turkey. She also resided in Königsberg, Marburg, and Frankfurt. After her husband's death in 1958 she made her home in Frankfurt. During a visit in Rome, she died on October 10, 1974.

Kaschnitz was the author of several novels; she also wrote poetry and radio plays. She received literary prizes, notably the Georg Büchner Prize of the German Academy for Language and Literature (1955) and the Immermann Prize for Literature (1957). In 1960–61 she lectured on poetics at the University of Frankfurt. *Liebe beginnt,* her first novel (1933), was well received and was praised by Ricarda Huch. During the 1930s, Kaschnitz wrote essays and poetry; one of her poems won first prize in the journal *Dame.* Another novel, *Elissa,* appeared in 1937. In 1946 she published a fictional rendering of a collection of Greek myths, reissued in paperback by dtv in 1975. Her reputation immediately after the war became fully established with the publication of several volumes of poetry: *Gedichte* (1947), *Totentanz und Gedichte zur Zeit* (1947), *Zukunftsmusik* (1950), *Ewige Stadt* (1952), and *Neue Gedichte* (1957). In her first collection of short stories, *Lange Schatten* (1960) she demonstrated her concise mastery of this genre. The critical-historical edition of her works in seven volumes was published by Insel Verlag, Frankfurt, in 1983.

It would be wrong to reduce the literary work of Kaschnitz to the topic of the anthropology of childhood. Yet throughout the stages of her work, in all of the genres she undertook (including biography and radio plays), we encounter a preoccupation with the nature of childhood depicted as a body of experience that continues to move parallel to maturity.

As early as 1938, just a few years after beginning her writing career, Kaschnitz composed a seven-stanza poem titled "Childhood." After describing the dual nature of joy and terror of childhood in concrete visual and auditory imagery, she concluded:

> It's still that way:
> Blossoms toss in the wind,
> The cuckoo calls in the forest,
> Yet the depth of pain and joy
> We never plumbed.

As late as 1973, one year before her death in Rome, in the context of quite another genre, the autobiographical reflections, *Orte (Places)*, she referred to another kind of childhood experience. Kaschnitz ironically observed in connection with her own only child, Costanza, that it may be worse for a child to grow up in a "good marriage" than with a set of "bad" parents. Having parents who always agree with one another deprives the child of any leverage or sympathetic side to play off against the other parent, and such "isolation" can hold its own terror.

In *The House of Childhood*, written during Kaschnitz's second stay in Rome (1953–56), the narrator is by no means thrilled about the prospect of encountering her childhood, because she suspects – only to be confirmed in the first stages or "lessons" of her encounter – that it was not a golden age at all. Second, and perhaps more important, Kaschnitz does not self-indulgently recall her childhood as a nostalgic trip into the past; instead her episodic encounter with childhood is a sleeves-rolled-up archaeological excavation into memory. As Wolfgang Hildesheimer, in an early review of this work, pointed out, Kaschnitz's artistic achievement is chiefly the subtle distinction of narrator from author. Even greater mastery of fictional technique and inventiveness can be seen in her conception of childhood as a place or building, the "H.O.C.," a kind of teaching museum and device for enhancing the imperfect capacity of memory. I do not dismiss interpretations of *The House of Childhood* as an elaborately disguised case history of psychotherapy as categorically as Elsbeth Pulver has done in her monograph on Kaschnitz. But Kaschnitz's dedication of *The House of Childhood* to her siblings ("Meinen Geschwistern zugeeignet") hints at additional, external memory aids which a single memory would be incapable of encompassing.

As has been pointed out by other commentators, *The House of Childhood* can also be seen as an elaboration of one of Kaschnitz's famous short stories, "The Fat Child" (1951). In this story Kaschnitz comes to terms with her adult disgust for herself as a phlegmatic, helpless, "caterpillar-like" creature.

Kaschnitz's own youth closely parallels that of her narrator's in *The House of Childhood*. What was it like to be a child in the years between 1901 and 1914? This she sketches with characteristic reticence in six paragraphs titled "When I Was a Child – Remembrances," published in the Christmas issue of *Rheinischer Merkur*, 1958, only two years after *The House of Childhood* appeared. Although Kaschnitz characterizes her social class as middle class ("bürgerlich"), it would be more accurate to refer to it as patrician. She was brought up in an old aristocratic family in the southwestern part of Germany and Alsace. Nevertheless, her characterization rings true: "When I was a child, middle-class parents were something lofty – distant gods in their own houses. One only entered when being asked."

In addition to describing very detailed vignettes of a childhood in the early part of the century, which ring true and at the same time expand our understanding of childhood and parenthood in general, the most distinctive strength of this fictional diary may lie in its startling contemporaneity and prophecy. The time of narration is not the late 1950s, but rather the late 1990s! Throughout the episodes surrounding the childhood encounters are references to such events as the extinction of horses and the elimination of such vestiges of civilized life as sidewalks. By means of these futuristic expansions, Kaschnitz's work of the 1950s anticipates the technological skepticism and the ecological dread so characteristic of late twentieth-century intellectual life. The very impetus for her reflections on being a child may have been the fear of nuclear holocaust alluded to in this work. Such fears found expression elsewhere in her work, notably in her well-known poem "Hiroshima" written in 1951.

The House of Childhood predates the publication of Philippe Aries's influential work *The History of Childhood* by four years. Notably, the subject of childhood emerged in the late 1950s as a new path of inquiry in social and cultural history. Since then, modern literary works as well as new editions of older works such as the new translations of the stories by the Brothers Grimm parallel the research in the social sciences. At the beginning of this exciting trend stands Marie Luise Kaschnitz's *The House of Childhood*.

HAL H. RENNERT